The Human Paradise

The Human Paradise

by
Nicolas Ségur

Translated, annotated and introduced by
Brian Stableford

A Black Coat Press Book

ISBN 978-1-61227-617-5. First Printing. May 2017. Published by Black Coat Press, an imprint of Hollywood Comics.com, LLC, P.O. Box 17270, Encino, CA 91416.
Printed in the United States of America.

TABLE OF CONTENTS

Introduction

The first of the two novellas by Nicolas Ségur making up the present volume, *Une Ile d'amour*, here translated as *An Isle of Amour*, was first published in Paris in 1921 by Eugène Fasquelle at the Bibliothèque Charpentier. The second, *Le Paradis des hommes*, here translated as *The Human Paradise*, was first published in 1930 by Albin Michel. As the brief introduction to the second item reveals, however, it was begun in 1918, emerging from discussions that the author had with Anatole France before the end of the Great War, and suffered a long interruption before the final version was written, apparently in 1929. It is evidently not merely a companion piece to *Une Ile d'amour*, on which the influence of the discussions in question becomes obvious with the aid of hindsight, but also a companion-piece of sorts of Anatole France's masterpiece *La Révolte des Anges* (1923; tr. as *The Revolt of the Angels*), on which the influence of the same discussion is similarly evident in retrospect, Satan's celebrated final speech in France's novel overlapping thematically with God's final message in *Le Paradis des hommes*.

The two novellas are the only works of futuristic fiction that Nicolas Ségur produced, and they contrast strongly with the rest of his output; the second, in particular was published at a time when the author had settled into a comfortable commercial rut, and it seems highly probable that Albin Michel—a publisher not known for his sympathy to futuristic fiction—only agreed to publish it as a favor to the author, whose other books were making him good money. Although the sales of two of the near-contemporary Albin Michel titles listed in the preliminary material of *Le Paradis des Hommes* are advertized as having sold thirty thousand copies, and the least of the four as having sold ten thousand, the copy I used for translation is marked "second thousand," and its pages were still uncut when I bought it, 86 years after publication, so that second thousand obviously did not sell out. That is, however, not an unusual fate for imaginative fiction of the period, when it was exceedingly marginal in the literary marketplace, and the wonder is not the book's commercial failure and subsequent fall into oblivion, but that fact that the author succeeded in persuading the publisher to issue it at all. It is probably safe to say, however, that Anatole France would have loved it, and would have been proud to have made some contribution to it.

"Nicolas Ségur" was born Nikolaos Episkopopolous on the Greek island of Zakynthos in 1874; he began his writing career as a journalist in Athens in the late 1890s, and published a number of books in Greek. In the early years of the 20th century, however, he moved to Paris and settled there permanently, eventually dying there in 1944, subsequently writing exclusively in French. He made the acquaintance of Anatole France not long after arriving in Paris and was taken under the latter's wing; one of his earliest French publications was a profile of the author published in *La Revue* in 1907. His conversations with Anatole France subsequently provided him with the material for three books, beginning with the best-selling *Conversations avec Anatole France ou Les Mélancolies de l'intelligence* (1925;

tr. as *Conversations with Anatole France*), published in the year after the great man's death.

Ségur's first volume in French was *Pages de Légende* [Pages of Legend] (1918), and his love of ancient Greek literature and myth is also reflected in his first novel, *Naïs au Miroir* [Nais at the Mirror] (1920), which had a preface by Anatole France, and in a sequel to the Odyssey, *Le Secret de Pénélope* [Penelope's Secret] (1922). Both of those novels sold tolerably well, as did *Une Ile d'amour*, which he wrote in between them, and even his fictitious philosophical monologue *M. Renan devant l'amour* [Ernest Renan on Amour] (1923) was subsequently advertised as having sold five thousand copies. From the publication of *La Belle Venise* [Beautiful Venice] (1924) onwards, however, the level of his success increased significantly as he found a profitable vein, redeploying the philosophical insights regarding the role of amour in human affairs deployed in *M. Renan devant l'amour* in a long series of contemporary novels exploring the problems and unfortunate side-effects of amorous passion, in a melodramatic and sometimes feverish fashion.

Ségur continued to write non-fiction alongside his novels and published a notable collection of essays on *La Génie Européen* [European Genius] in 1926. He also attempted to continue writing philosophical fiction, producing *Le Cinquième évangile: Saint François d'Assise* [The Fifth Evangelist: St. Francis of Assisi] (1925) and *Platon cherche l'amour* [Plato in Search of Amour] (1926), but the contrast between the sales of those volume and his contemporary erotica, as in the case of *Le Paradis des hommes*, must have been discouraging to him as well as his publishers, and throughout the 1930s, almost all of his fiction followed a pattern that became increasingly stereotyped. He died in 1944.

Un Ile d'amour is particularly interesting as an addition to a sequence of French utopian novels that attempted to get to grips with the thorny question of how best to organize sexual relations in a utopia, and what the social consequences would be of instituting a system of "free love"; earlier novels in the sequence, at least some of which Ségur had presumably read, included Paul Adam's *Lettres de Malaisie* (1898; tr. as "Letters from Malaisie"),[1] André Couvreur's *Caresco, surhomme* (1904; tr. as *Caresco, Superman*),[2] Han Ryner's *Les Pacifiques* (1914; tr. as "The Pacifists")[3] and Marcel Rouff's *Voyage au monde à l'envers* (1920: tr. as *Journey to the Inverted World*).[4]

Ségur's novel makes an interesting addition to that series in terms of its treatment of sexual relations on the island on Pamphilia in the twenty-first century, particularly in its modification of the careful separation between promiscuous sex and eugenically-planned reproduction featured in Couvreur's novel. However, it also has other interesting features, some of which hark back to Plato's *Republic*, most interestingly the internment within special asylums on the island of victims of passionate amour—here viewed as a kind of mental illness—on the one hand, and intellectuals on the other, poets, philosophers and scientists all being forbidden to

---

[1] Included in *The Humanisphere*, Black Coat Press, ISBN 978-1-61227-511-6.

[2] Black Coat Press, ISBN 978-1-61227-254-2.

[3] Included in *The Human Ant*, Black Coat Press, ISBN 978-1-61227-323-5.

[4] Black Coat Press, ISBN 978-1-61227-039-5.

mingle with the happily innocent islanders. The Swiftian satire of the latter chapter of the novel is somewhat reminiscent Gulliver's visit to the Academy of Lagado, but it does raise a serious question as to whether utopia is really a fit environment for intellectuals, and whether their presence within it might be dangerously corrupting. The novella is one of the few examples of a proposed ideal state from which its own author would automatically be banished.

The notion of the inherent dangers of intellectual acuity and its potential deleterious effects on the prospects of human happiness is reproduced in *Le Paradis des hommes*, a more scathingly sarcastic satire closely akin to Anatole France's paradoxical fantasies in terms of the delight it takes in challenging received notions and overturning them by extrapolation to absurdity. It is, in one sense, a magnification of the classic fairy tale theme of granting three wishes—which are usually employed in an unwise fashion—but it moves the motif into a more portentous imaginative arena by having God offer to grant wishes expressed unanimously by the entirety of humankind. The wishes voiced, although two of them, at least, seem highly plausible candidates for inclusion on such a list, are carefully extrapolated in such a way as to suggest that however effective individuals might be at screwing up their wishes, a committee composed of the whole human race could do a far more comprehensive job.

The opening chapters of *Les Paradis des hommes* are very obviously a product of the experience of the Great War of 1914-18 and the change in consciousness that experience wrought in French society. Although its initial tragic consciousness is modified by the long gap between the writing of the first fragments and their eventual filling out into a coherent narrative, that distance takes some of the edge off the mordant humor, and does not affect its essential blackness and rueful philosophy. (The war is always cited in the text as the 1914 war, or simply as "1914," which might reflecting the fact that much of it was written before the date of the armistice as known; the same practice is also followed in "Un Ile d'amour," however, raising the possibility that that novel too as written, or at least begun, before the armistice.)

Individually fascinating, the juxtaposition of the two works and their judgments regarding the suitability of humans for living a utopian or paradisal existence adds an extra dimension of interest to them, and must make lovers of imaginative fiction regret that Ségur was not able to follow his evident inclinations in that direction further—although that has always been the common fate of writers of that stripe. Although we do not live on Pamphilia, and certainly do not share the bliss of its islanders, the literary marketplace has always succeeded in interning the majority of writers possessed of adventurous imaginative verve and scope, and usually in silencing them after a few signs of rebellious intelligence...but not always permanently.

The translation of *Une Ile d'amour* was made from the London Library's copy of the 1921 edition. As noted above, the translation of *Le Paradis des hommes* was made from a copy of the Albin Michel edition.

Brian Stableford

AN ISLE OF AMOUR

I. The Stranger

King Henri leaned over, extended his hand, and then closed it abruptly, trapping a green grasshopper that had launched itself over the tender grass, avid for dew.

The King remained motionless, contemplating the supple and graceful insect, the form of which participates in those of the lyre and the bow.

The morning was beautiful and the gardens embalmed. One felt troubled by the beauties of spring there, and breathed I know not what voluptuous breath, which softened the body and rendered the pleasure of living sweeter.

Henri turned to his chamberlain, who was following him at a distance.

"We're two various and impenetrable worlds, this grasshopper and I. It's maddened by fear, bewildered and grieved to find itself imprisoned in my hand. It can have no suspicion of the fact that I'm its friend, or what a keen wonder it inspires in me."

"It desires, on the contrary to leap far away from Your Majesty."

"In sum, it's right," said King Henri. "In spite of my intentions, I'm incapable of doing it the slightest good, while I can do it all harm. In those conditions, my intervention in its destiny is redoubtable in every way."

And the king opened his fingers, liberating the insect, which traced a rapid curve and was lost in the midst of the verdure.

"How mild the air is!" said the King then, stopping before a field of anemones offering its first fruits to renewal. "Every instant that goes by appears to be the best in life."

In fact, nature appeared to be bearing the seal of perfection. A kind of ecstatic joy emanated from everything.

"It's necessary to tear ourselves away from these charms, Probus," said the King. "It's time to go back inside. If my duties leave me enough leisure, I'll go for a leisurely stroll along the river bank later."

"You're giving an audience in your tribunal today," the chamberlain objected.

"Let's hope that no one presents themselves there. The people of the island are too happy to quarrel, or to complain. For three weeks there hasn't been a single case to judge, and you'll see that it will be the same today."

When they reached the palace, as they climbed the three pink marble steps of the perron, the chamberlain addressed the daily request to his master: "Sire, what should be done with the young woman who came into your bed yesterday evening?"

"Her name's Georgette," said the King. "She's very young and very healthy. But all things considered, as her soul isn't warm, order that she be sent to the Insemination Palace."

The chamberlain bowed.

"Come and find me in the Queen's apartments," said King Henri, dismissing him with a gesture and going into his apartments.

A valet immediately brought him breakfast on a silver tray.

"Has General Xenius come down yet?" asked King Henri.

"Yes, Sire," replied the valet, bowing. "I saw him coming out of Her Majesty the Queen's apartments."

Henri ate diligently and frugally, and then they went, in accordance with his matinal habit, to see his wife.

On the staircase he met Georgette, who was going away, accompanied by the chamberlain.

"Adieu, child," said the monarch, pinching her cheek and smiling at her. "Don't be sorry about going to the Insemination Palace. Life there is more tranquil."

Georgette bowed, trying to mask her visible discontentment.

Having arrived at his wife's apartments, King Henri knocked and went in.

The Queen, occupied in her toilette, was consulting a large mirror, which reflected a ravishing image, with satisfaction.

Anne of Pamphilia had a tall, calm and grave beauty. Her body, scarcely attained by a slight plumpness, moved comfortably in a dark red dress fissured at the top, allowing her agreeably-turned shoulder to appear, and the rounded and delicate birth of her breasts. Her face was framed by blonde hair, and her profound eyes seemed to reflect restful and fresh images.

"Did you have a good night, my dear Anne?" said the King, approaching affectionately, while gazing at his wife.

"Excellent," the Queen replied. "Yesterday evening after your departure, we continued chatting with the general. He's witty, and knows a lot about agriculture. We went to bed quite late."

"Everything's going well, then," said the King, sitting down. "It's a fine day, the fields are getting visibly greener, and the fragrance of the flowers of the almond trees reaches all the way here from the confines of the island."

"I intend to take a walk in that direction through the Lovers' Park," the Queen said.

"As for me, if circumstances permit, I'll go down to the river. In this season there are exceedingly red fish with nacreous undersides. One thinks that one is contemplating the sun when one pulls them out of the water."

"We might run into one another on the way."

At that moment, someone knocked softly on the door.

"Come in," said the King.

It was the chamberlain, who had come to fetch him.

"It's past eleven, Sire. You're awaited in the Tribunal."

"There are cases to judge, then?" asked Henri, slightly disappointed.

"Only one. It's a matter of a dispute between and islander and a stranger."

"A stranger? How did he get here? That's odd. Let's go see, quickly."

The King went into his bedroom in order to exchange his simple costume for ceremonial attire, then seized a cane with an ivory handle, an insignia of royalty, and went into the tribunal hall.

It was entirely hung with faded velvet. On the back wall there were a few discreetly-embroidered inscriptions, devoid of order but not of harmony.

Justice is a frightful necessity.

Judgment is the affirmation of the superiority of the multitude to individuals.

We shall be just as long as we are the stronger. On days of good health we shall also try to be clement.

The King took his place beneath the consecrated awning.

"Introduce the plaintiffs," he said.

Two men and a woman came in. The woman, who was about twenty-five, displayed a becoming beauty, with keen eyes, a slightly olive complexion and mobile nostrils as delicately carved as gems. She wore the customary costume of the island, coquettishly: a transparent tunic, tightened around the hips by a broad yellow silk belt whose knot spread out laterally.

One of the two men was evidently her husband, and was holding her by the hand. An ample velvet garment made of a single piece of fabric covered him in a dignified manner. He appeared to be heading for middle age, and his beautiful beard and bright eyes inspired benevolence.

The adversary, elegantly clad in a European costume in blue cloth, was scarcely twenty, and the expression of his regular features presented the alliance of energy and mildness typical of Latins.

"Sire, my name in Jules Brandin and I live at the southern extremity of the island, near Paradisal Bay," said the islander, bowing before the King. "The day before yesterday, this stranger, who does not lack politeness and whose courage I esteem, came down in his airplane a hundred meters from our house."

"How were you able to reach our little island, Monsieur?" said the King, interrupting the deposition and addressing the stranger with interest. "Pamphilia is isolated in the southern Pacific. Boats never call here because we're a long way from any commercial route and only maintain communication with the Marquesas. Even those communications are widely spaced and restricted. It's been more than five years since I've seen a single stranger here. Where have you come from with your airplane?"

"Paris, Sire."

"You're a Parisian?" asked the King.

"Not exactly. I'm a Burgundian, but I always reside in Paris."

"And you've undertaken such a long voyage?"

"I'm flying an airplane constructed expressly for distant exploration. Coming from Patagonia, I had hoped to reach Australia without touching land...but I ran out of fuel..."

"I'm glad to converse with a Frenchman, Monsieur, and to have news of my former homeland."

"You're originally from France, Sire?"

"Yes, I'm French, and I'm only hiring myself out," the King replied, graciously. "My family is from Poitou...but I'm digressing from the matter at hand," he went on, while his face darkened. "How is it that I see you cited before my tribunal? What is it that divides you and the excellent Jules Brandin, who lives in the most beautiful part of my island? He surely hasn't refused you hospitality?"

"He has, on the contrary, accorded it to me in the broadest and most unexpected fashion. I am more surprised by it, in fact, than anything else that has happened to me on your beautiful island."

"Perhaps it would be more appropriate if Brandin explains to me the cause that brings you before me," said the King.

"The airplane," the islander then recounted, "touched down as dusk was approaching. It was already getting a little cold. I hastened to prepare a good dinner and I invited the stranger to warm himself at my hearth."

"You were obliging and generous," the Frenchman put in.

"After dinner," Brandin continued, "he told me his name, recounted his voyage, and we talked for a long time about his homeland. Then I asked him, politely, whether he found my wife Amanda pretty, and, on his affirmative response, I conducted him to his bedroom. Then I sent Amanda to him. She went again the following day to keep him company at the hour of the siesta. But imagine my surprise, O King, when, on questioning her, wanting to assure myself that she had been meekly pliant to the desires of our guest, I learned things that offended me extremely. I shall leave her the care of confessing them and I ask you for justice."

"Speak, my daughter," said the King, encouraging the beautiful Amanda with a gesture and inviting her to come closer. "With what have you to reproach the stranger?"

"I reproach him, Sire, with having spoken to me about amour with insistence," replied Amanda, blushing.

"He spoke to you about amour? No, that's not possible," said the King, poorly impressed and darting a disapproving glance at the Frenchman.

"Yes, Sire, I'm telling the pure truth," the young woman continued. "Instead of honestly sharing with me the pleasure that I accorded to him, he never stopped asking me whether I loved him amorously, if I could consecrate my thoughts to him and if I would always retain his memory."

"Is that true?" asked the King, turning toward the stranger, sadly.

"It's scrupulously exact," confessed the latter. "But what do you find reprehensible about it? When I entered my host's house I noticed Madame's beauty, and I was touched by it. Respectful of the laws of hospitality, however, I did not believe it permissible to look at her. Great was my astonishment when, with her husband's consent, she came to undress in my bedroom and offered herself to me. She expressed herself in an adulterated and particular French, the same that I have heard with surprise throughout the country. I obtained an extreme pleasure with her and scarcely thought of abandoning myself to sleep. I thought I was the victim of a dream in feeling her quiver in my arms and respond eloquently to my caresses.

"Then I wanted to know whether she loved me as I loved her, whether she wanted to prolong the too-brief hours that we spent together, and whether I had any chance of occupying her memory as much as she had invaded mine. I believed that in aspiring to something more than her body, in wanting to penetrate more deeply into her inner being, I was only appreciating the gift that she had accorded me. I was in any case, far from thinking that I was offending her, and I scarcely understood her distress and disturbance. Even less can I disentangle the causes of her husband's irritation. He insisted that I come with him to present myself before you."

Jules Brandin wanted to speak, but the King stopped him with a gesture.

"There's no need to add anything," he said. "Right is on your side and your guest's only excuse is his evident ignorance of the laws of our island. He has shown himself to be presumptuous in wanting to imprint his image for eternity in the heart and soul of this charming woman, whose body alone was offered to him. A stranger to our mores, he had no suspicion of the grave punishments that one incurs here when one pronounces the redoubtable name of Amour lightly."

"In fact, I was unaware of all that," said the stranger, gallantly. "If, nevertheless I have offended this man, for whom I nourish nothing but gratitude, I am ready for any reparation."

"I only demand justice," said Brandin.

"What is your name?" the King asked the stranger.

"Pierre Fortier, Sire."

"Well, Monsieur Fortier, you will not refuse, I hope, to tell your host that you greatly regret the wrong that you have tried to do him by inducing amour in his wife."

"But I scarcely understand that wrong."

"Apologize anyway; you'll understand later."

And, when Fortier had made his apologies the King went on, addressing Brandin: "I cannot, properly speaking, punish him. As a stranger he is under my protection, and I answer, in a way, for his security. Then again, he has only sinned out of ignorance. But to compensate you for the damage that you have experienced, I award you the rosette of the Order of the Silver Pigeon."

Brandin's face was radiant with contentment.

"Go in peace with your wife," added the King. "I shall give orders for someone to watch over Monsieur Fortier's airplane. He will reside in my palace henceforth."

And, while pressing an electric button, the King said: "I hope, Monsieur Fortier, that you're not thinking of leaving us immediately.

"I couldn't, Sire, even if I wanted to," the young man replied, smiling. "First, I need to find fuel."

"You'll find it easily, but there's no hurry. Nothing would give me greater pleasure than to offer you long hospitality."

"I'm sensible of the honor that you're doing me, and I'll gladly remain in Pamphilia for a few days. Curiosity and pleasure engage me to do so. I ought, however, to confess to you, since you're so indulgent toward me, that I am going from one surprise to another. At every moment I dread infringing laws and customs that remain inexplicable to me."

"I shall satisfy your curiosity, if you remain with me for three or four days. You can talk to me about your homeland and I'll explain the origins and habits of my kingdom to you."

Turning toward the valet who was waiting by the door, he said: "Tell the Queen that I'll have the pleasure of introducing her to a young Frenchman, a newcomer to the island."

Then he took out his watch. "We have lunch at one o'clock," he told Fortier. The Prince and the Princesses should already have returned. Do you like fishing?"

"Passionately, Sire," replied the young man, without conviction.

"Then you can accompany me this afternoon to the river bank and I'll explain to you in detail what it's necessary for you to know about Pamphilia.

And the King, having perceived through the window an amazon descending from a horse, called to her: "Monique! Monique!"

He turned to the stranger. "This is my younger daughter. Go and take a stroll around the garden with her until lunch-time." He smiled. "Above all, I beg you, don't talk to her about amour. You've already seen that it's the worst of improprieties in Pamphilia."

II. Pamphilia

The King sat down next to Pierre Fortier on a thick carpet that the chamberlain had ordered to be laid out on the bank of the cheerful river.

He baited his hooks and cast adroitly. Then he began his story.

"The existence of the kingdom of Pamphilia, which causes you so much amazement, dates back a little more than eighty years. My grandfather, Henri the Great, was the founder and first king. He was thirty-nine years old when he left Paris in 1931 and came to settle on this island. A hundred and seventy-three people accompanied him, adherent to his ideas and ready to share his destiny. Henri the Great suffered painfully from a chronic neurasthenia and had a fortune of eight hundred millions that his father, the engineer Bouvallon, amassed rapidly by inventing a mixture of rubber and silica that permitted the pneumatic tires of vehicles to last indefinitely."

"Indeed, the Bouvallon brand is still highly esteemed in France," Fortier put in.

"So much the better," replied the King, politely. "But to understand fully the considerations that determined Henri Bouvallon to abandon Paris and come to found this modest kingdom, it's necessary to know that he had a philosophical mind and that his unhealthy temperament disposed him to meditation. The bloody conflicts that had devastated and almost destroyed Europe in the first quarter of the twentieth century had augmented his aversion for the civilized. In his youth he had published a brief work on *The Profound Causes of Social Degeneration* and another on *The End of Races*. His essential ideas were that the European world was perishing by virtue of a excess of thought and refinement, that our bodies were becoming incapable of supporting the transformations of the modern brain and that the three Latin scourges, art, letters and amour, would end up reckoning with the human plant.

"If I had had enough muscular strength and healthy tissue, he wrote in his memoirs, *perhaps I would have continued to live the life of everyone else, seeking honors, devouring space, living for pleasures, making sterile speeches about abstractions and collecting without measure the frivolous gifts that every day brings to Parisians. But I was weak, amour was no longer anything to me but disappointment, and I was beginning to experience the sensation of being sated without ever being satisfied. That is why I resolved to devote myself to my descendants, at least saving my posterity and that of my friends who would consent to follow me.*

"After that, my ancestor conceived and nourished the project of fleeing modern dissolution and regenerating his race. As he had not only inherited the fortune but also the enterprising genius of his father, he founded a limited company, gave lectures, converted his friends, attracted new followers by speech and the pen, and then chose his island and purchased it. In March 1931 a colony of a hundred and seventy-three people of the male sex, belonging to several nations but in which the Latin element predominated, landed on the idle of Pamphilia. The colonists were accompanied by a few women, mostly mistresses, because the legitimate wives, except the poorest, refused to go with their husbands.

"It's necessary that I tell you that this little isle, formerly pagan and prosperous, had been civilized in the seventeenth century by the Spaniards, and then Christianized by the Jesuit fathers, which the population was unable to resist. At the moment when Henri Bouvallon made the acquisition of it the island was completely civilized and Christian, but deserted.

"My grandfather also admitted to his colony a few robust and beautiful women from neighboring islands in order to fortify the enfeebled bloodlines, and the population of Pamphilia, which originally amounted to about three hundred persons of both sexes increased rapidly, and in proportions unknown in any other country. Today my kingdom counts three thousand inhabitants. But how can you not have heard mention of that escapade of my grandfather's, which caused such a lot of fuss at the time? Henri the Great was represented, it appears, in the revues of all the petty Parisian theaters, journalists came all the way here to interview him and I possess thirty-two ditties written in his honor."

"In Paris, as you know, everything happens and is forgotten rapidly," Fortier replied. "I must confess that I was completely unaware of the colonization of Pamphilia, and that I located the island with the aid of a map."

"I won't talk about the prosperity of my country," the King continued, after having pulled from the water, triumphantly, a mobile and graceful fish that was flapping its fins madly. "There has never been any epidemic and there are few lawsuits. What is more, there is no Pamphilian history, to the extent that the kings here are alternately named Henri and François without any other designation, since there is hardly any necessity to distinguish them. They are from the Bouvallon family, for the island, purchased entirely with our money, is our property. The reigns resemble one another and are all confused in perfect happiness.

"In default of Pamphilian history and notable events, however, I can tell you the sage regulations by means of which Henri the Great succeeded in fortifying his people and establishing them on durable bases.

"*Repose the brain, abolish the anxieties of the soul, accord the body the greatest sum of pleasure compatible with health*: that is the triple objective of his laws.

"First he thought about the material ease of the colonists. The climate and nature of the soil make Pamphilia strangely akin to the Society Islands; that tells you that one lives here under a special celestial protection and in a sort of paradise. The island produces what is necessary to live reasonably, and the coconut palm, the banana tree with giant leaves, the areca palm, the breadfruit tree, the grapefruit and the mango tree furnish us with bread, fruits, beverages and clothing. The Pamphilians possess flocks and fields but they do little labor and spend the greater part of their days in their pleasures, since the commerce in island products and the carpet factories that Henri the Great established in the south of the isle easily bring in all the sums necessary for the prosperity and embellishment of the kingdom.

"I beg you now to believe that, although we are severed from thought and far from civilization, we do not live like savages. The founder, who liked material ease, tolerated and introduced into the colony all the proven and inoffensive fruits of science. We do not employ steam, condemned because of the heavy aspect and polluting nature of locomotives, but we make abundant use of electricity. We work all metals except for gold, the high price of which seems to us to be inexcusable. And although the arts are suspect to us, we nevertheless rest our eyes gladly on certain indisputable masterpieces of the past that decorate and enhance our meeting-places.

We have also conserved for our distraction the phonograph and Italian music, which is essentially melodic. There is no need to tell you that alcohol, coffee and anesthetics, without being banned—they are granted, on the contrary, to citizens during festivals and celebrations—are severely and exclusively for private usage.

"Without lingering over details that you will grasp yourself during your walks, however, I shall arrive immediately at the much more important radical reforms that my grandfather instituted with regard to mores.

"First of all, in order to be spiritually tranquilized, we have a religion. By its essential practices it is confounded with those of the old occidental world. In sum, King Henri only innovated with regard to two points. Firstly, he abolished the clergy, reserving the unique priesthood to the king, and secondly, he attenuated and modified the prohibitions relative to the relations of the sexes. We believe in principle in another life but we are urgently invited by the law not to think about it. Any Pamphilian who, at the end of the year, swears before the mayor to having thought fewer than three times about the divine nature, the origins of the earth, the destiny of the world and the immortality of the soul receives a large gourd of wine and the small decoration of the Golden Butterfly. We have also reestablished the admirable institution of indulgences. The King, who disposes of them, remits twice a year the sins of all citizens whose general conduct has been identified as good.

"My grandfather also thought about military organization, and we have an army. Properly speaking, it is no use, since we live in security from invasions and wars and we maintain the best of relations with the other Pacific islands. But precisely because the army is not materially useful, we surround it with all possible respect. It augments the prestige of the government and encourages the citizen to revere the laws.

"As for military service, it does not last long but remains fairly dangerous because of its conditions. In fact, the great maneuvers that take place at the beginning of every bissextile year, putting adverse regiments seriously at odds, degenerate into veritable battles and cause considerable losses, Henri the Great wanted it thus, and neither my father nor I has dared to reform his regulations. Having seen the war of 1914 at close range, he professed that there are certain human instincts whose expansion and exercise it is necessary to respect.

"*The sentiment of danger and the necessity of self-defense from time to time, temper the strength of the individual, preventing softness and relieving the soul*, he wrote in his *Motivated Code*. *If you do not have decreed wars, you will have riots, which is worse*. And he added in conversation that, the majority of Pamphilians being European in origin, they necessarily have certain heredities that imply the need for a preventive bleeding from time to time. 'It is by revolutions, and by dint of shedding blood that Europe seems to regenerate itself and persist,' he concluded.

"As for the law, it functions with mildness. In the fear of possible abuses, the laws are exclusively applied by me. Amour, the idea of honor, competition between rivals, the vanity of acquisition and the desire to *arrive* being, as you have seen for yourself, unknown in Pamphilia, misdemeanors are rare. Petty thefts of fruits, infractions of the policing of the streets, excesses of merriment and a few cases of smuggling are the only misdeeds that are committed on the island. The penalties are also light, but efficacious and, I even dare say, all powerful. I exclude culpable males temporarily from participation in our festivals, which occasions the privation of sensual pleasures and the use of narcotics.

"As for women, I habitually sentence them to walk naked in the streets for a certain time. That punishment is not aimed at their modesty, since amorous matters are conducted overtly here and nudity is not reprehensible, but it afflicts their coquetry. Naked women are neglected on Pamphilia, firstly because they no longer offer the attraction of mystery and curiosity, which is the departure point of all carnal desires, and also because they find it impossible to ornament themselves, to increase and enfever their charms with the aid of varied colors and fashionable artifices. The wound of fashion, in spite of the laws originally formulated by Henri the Great, cannot be avoided, and like Solon, who was obliged to recall the courtesans he had previously banished, my grandfather was obliged to reestablish the liberty of titivation.

"I ought to add that in my capacity as supreme judge I apply the law as I see fit, without founding myself on texts. We fear procedure, knowing that the law rests on a single principle, that of force, which was created to defend associations, and has the destiny of being incessantly violated by the great and dominators, and that it ought to confess its obscure and iniquitous origins if it does not want to appear absurd and cruel.

"But the great reform of this land, the imperishable glory of Henri the Great, was the condemnation of logical thought and the isolation of beings who exhibit a dangerous development of the imaginative faculties.

"*Every exceptional being ought to be set apart and not trouble the tranquility of average humanity by his actions, his desires or his dreams.* Such was my grandfather's firm opinion on this subject; he remained convinced that the end of all great peoples occurred by virtue of a disequilibrium between the brain and the body, straying outside natural laws, speculative and logical hyperactivity.

"The role of thought, he said, word for word in the first article of the Pamphilian constitution, *is to aid human beings to make a place in the natural environment and usefully transform the external world. As soon as thought agitates in abstraction, without any immediate and material object, it deviates dangerously from its direction. To maintain the health and equilibrium of all vital functions, and even more, to assure human wellbeing, it is necessary to forbid absolutely any speculative straying. Except for those of my subjects who are recognized as abnormal and who will, in consequence, be isolated and treated as scholars or poets, the remainder— by which I mean the totality of true Pamphilians—will carefully avoid any philosophical, scientific or literary reading, and any artistic occupation. They will also abstain from discussion, which is formally prohibited, since the King is always there to clarify questions and resolve problems. 'The Lord's day,' which will recur once a week, will permit the measured experience, in common, of certain artifices of civilization. The rest of the time, Pamphilians must be light-minded, distracted by natural beauties, as little reflective and given to worry as the growing grass, a bird in flight and a chicken motionlessly brooding its eggs.*

"Such is, essentially, the basis of the social edifice created by my grandfather. So, printing is almost unknown to us and I am the only one to read the books and periodicals that I receive from Europe in order to keep up to date with the progress of the world. My subjects, having learned in school certain facts useful to life and métiers, not longer read anything but what relates to the rites of religion and customs.

"I shall renounce expressing to you what sort of regeneration the penury of books and what physical and moral freshness the total absence of newspapers produces in Pamphilia. It's miraculous. The regulation of thought and the even wiser and more radical regulation of amorous matters, about which it remains to me to talk to you, are the two solid foundations on which all the isle's prosperity is raised. If the Golden Age reigns in Pamphilia it is to those two causes that we owe it."

The King placed in a wicker basket the few fish that he had obtained with the aid of patience and cunning. Then, taking his guest's arm, he went along the path that led to the palace.

"I don't have time to explain to you in detail the extreme and admirable organization of everything related to sexual attraction. You will stay here for a few days, so you will have the opportunity to see for yourself the remarkable accomplishments achieved in that regard. For the moment, it will be sufficient for me to tell you that Henri the Great conceived sexual pleasure and the procreation of children as separate and distinct matters. Sexual intercourse, an inexhaustible source of contentment, a calming recreation, a necessary mirage that causes the evils of existence to be forgotten, remains the inalienable privilege of the individual Pamphilian. As for generation, a capital function that concerns not so much the citizen as the city, ought to be directed in accordance with immutable and scientific principles, outside of all illusion, all apparent attraction and above fugitive sympathies or temporary proprieties.

Pamphilians will regulate themselves in perfect liberty with regard to everything that concerns their own pleasure, wrote Henri the Great in his code. And, indeed, no prohibition shackles the relations between the sexes on the island. On the other hand, that which relates to future citizens, that which interests the very destiny of the race and the future of the island, it is not individuals but us, the governors, who take care of it. Our efforts, our thoughts, our greatest sacrifices have been directed at all times toward that principal problem. And I dare say that no country in the world surpasses or equals us in that matter."

"You've talked to me about pleasure and procreation, but isn't all that favored or hindered by amour?" asked Fortier.

"Amour?" said the King.

"Yes, amorous sentiment, amorous passion..."

The sovereign's face darkened.

"The case of amour is anticipated. We'll talk about it at length another day. In any case, know at present that amour is fortunately rare in Pamphilia. We avoid it as much as we can; the facile access to pleasure and the extreme ease that reigns in mores restricts its ravages. You will see luminous signs at every street corner that carry the capital injunction that commences the national anthem: "Pamphilians, avoid amour!"

They had arrived at the door of the palace.

Dusk was extending slowly, and everything was taking on violet tints.

"Someone will take you to your apartment," Henri went on. "This evening, after dinner, and all tomorrow morning, I'll be busy verifying the kingdom's finances. I do that work once a year, assisted by four American bankers, fine bloodhounds, who sniff out silver naturally and are excellent at making it fructify. What exquisite senses for temporal things men of that nation have! To

33

my great regret, therefore, I cannot see you again until tomorrow afternoon. Then I shall take you to visit the Insemination Palace. Until then you're free to stroll around the isle and dispose of your time as you wish.

And as Pierre Fortier thanked him, warmly and expressed his admiration for everything sage and strange that he had heard, the King said: "You'll see the island and judge it for yourself. What is remarkable is the charm and naturalness of the Pamphilian race. When one thinks that from a few alcoholic and debilitated Europeans, who were in the process of brooding general paralysis, we have extracted so much beauty and vigor, one is wonderstruck!"

As they went into the palace, the King addressed his guest again:

"Listen, my dear Monsieur Fortier. You can't remain alone all the time I leave you at liberty, and in any case, it's not in the usages of the country to walk without company. People go around here in couples. The Queen's duties create multiple obligations, but there are my daughters, Princesses Adelaide and Monique, whom you know. Which do you choose for your friend?"

"Oh, Sire!"

"Respond without artifice. Have you not understood that our moral concepts differ from yours?"

"The two princesses, since you permit me to express myself on that subject, are the most perfectly beautiful young women that it has ever been given to me to see thus far," Fortier replied, enthusiastically.

"Would you prefer Adelaide, who is the elder?" said the King, with gentle persistence.

"I find her ravishing. And as for Mademoiselle Monique, she has inexpressible charms."

"Is it Monique who pleases you more?"

"I confess it."

"Then I grant you Monique. You'll be the first man she's approached.

"I swear, Sire, to respect the Princess."

"Don't do that, Monsieur, don't do that!" exclaimed the King. "It would not be viewed well in my family or in the land. Why, moreover, dissemble, lie and repress all desire? On the contrary, deploy your appetites, only respect yourself, as long as you're in Pamphilia, I implore you. You'll have time to don your mask again when you return to Europe in a few days' time."

And as it was announced that dinner was served, the King said, joyfully: "Let's go eat!"

III. The Insemination Palace

"How sweetly the Lady of the Water speaks!" said Princess Monique, raising herself up slightly and lending an ear to the sound.

She was lying alongside Pierre Fortier on a mobile lace of lianas, near the cascading spring.

Midday was spreading everywhere the torpor, the delightful somnolence that loosens corporeal chains and steals souls away from the present. The cane-toads were whistling with desire, the cicadas exultant, and in, the distance, the palm-trees and tamarisks were agitating with inexpressible softness.

Finding himself next to that primitive and docile child since the previous day, Pierre Fortier thought he was traversing the temeritous improbabilities of a dream.

He therefore responded to her remark: "Do springs truly have a soul?"

"Everything that sings must have a soul," said the Princess.

"Aren't you afraid of sensing so many living things around you?"

"By day I'm never afraid. Nature loves us and the sun is good. It's the darkness of the night that seems malevolent, and the sea when it's angry. People also sometimes inspire fear in me. Thus, yesterday evening, you frightened me by squeezing me in your arms for the first time. However, since then, you please me more."

"Would you sing me this morning's song again?" said Fortier.

"Gladly! I'm ready to do anything that's agreeable to you."

"Sing, then, Monique."
In a soft and caressant voice, she commenced:

Madame Ant, oh, Madame Ant,
You walk like a silkworm!
Oh, how you trot!
Oh, how you trot!
Ah la la! Ah la la!

Those words devoid of significance seemed nevertheless to express all the juvenile impatience, all the ardor and all the tenderness of Monique. On emerging from her lips, they acquired a strange and warm vibration.

As he gazed at that graceful body, abandoned to repose, Fortier recalled the singular circumstances in which Monique had belonged to him.

The previous evening, at table, the Queen had confirmed her husband's promise by telling the young woman that she should go with the stranger and reside with him.

At that moment they were eating custard-apples with the aid of little ivory spoons and, in Fortier's memory, the perfume of the tender flesh of the fruit was forever linked with the soft and unembarrassed gaze that Monique had directed at him when she heard her mother's instruction. How beautiful the young woman had been at that moment! Under the electric light that illuminated the sumptuous table, her fresh complexion with amber gleams was animated by fugitive flashes of red. The gaze that traversed the double caress of the long lashes, and the tender and pert mouth, dazzled and stirred Fortier

Once the dinner was over, Monique had come to find him in his room and, at the first private caresses, had shown surprise, and was then delighted by the pleasure that visited her.

"You kiss has the perfume of cherry blossom," she had said to the man. "My sister Adelaide's kisses, the only ones I've known thus far, are nothing compared to yours."

Then she had begun to babble incomprehensible words, like a child.

"What are you doing, Monique?" Fortier said to her.

"I'm praying to the Lord to conserve you in life."

He was astonished to see so much simplicity in her, and also to observe that the clear knowledge of carnal things had not harmed her candor. He compared her to savant and expert European virgins, steeped in flirtation, incessantly assailed by male desire, only half-defending themselves against his caresses, apparently intact and intimately corrupted, like certain beautiful fruits that a worm has emptied inside.

Monique was soon asleep in Pierre's arms, spreading her pure breath over his neck. Then, in the morning, nimble, cheerful and happy, she extended her mouth to him again, avidly and voluptuously.

When they got up she promptly put on her tunic and invited him to go for a walk with her.

"I'd like to do you the honors of our garden," she said.

Throughout the walk he was astonished to see her in perpetual intelligence with earthly things, agile, loquacious and mischievous, running an inviting him to catch her, slipping out of his arms and then teasingly offering her cheeks to be kissed. She picked roses with which to decorate him; she touched butterflies lightly without wanting to seize them, and seemed to make life into a perpetual communion with nature.

Their repose was interrupted by the coming of the King, who inquired solicitously about Fortier's health and the manner in which he had employed his time.

"I've been walking and I'm happy," the latter replied, blushing.

"We're very content with one another," added Monique, more frankly. "The sun has never seemed so bright to me as it does today."

"Now you ought to let us depart," the King said to his daughter, who meekly kissed Pierre and drew away.

Henri led his guest along the shady pathways of the town. "If you like, we'll go to visit the Palace of Insemination," he said to him. "In the same way that the Gardens of Pleasure, which you'll see later, are designed to make life forgotten and caress the senses, the temple consecrated to the future is an austere place, deprived of all softness, far from any idea of lightness."

They penetrated into the center of the island and stopped in front of a large square building, which respired the simplicity and amplitude typical of ancient architecture.

"In accordance with the conception of Henri the Great, this edifice is a true Spartan temple," the King explained. "Let's linger for a few moments on the periphery, for, before going in I want to explain certain things to you that appear to me to be necessary to the comprehension of what you're about to see."

And, going slowly along the marble colonnade, the King spoke to his guest thus:

"My grandfather's dream was to found one of those Fortunate Isles of which Greek and Breton legend

speaks. And as he knew that happiness resides essentially on health and corporeal plenitude, he first applied his
genius to the solution of the problem of children. To surround procreation with particular cares, to favor the integrity and the success of generations to come, to extract
his companions from neurosis and decadence by crossing them with beautiful indigenes, to match individuals,
to select unions, to fortify the race, such were his primary occupations.

Although my grandfather neglected European science is its other applications, he followed it step by step
and profited from its acquisitions when it was a matter of
the amelioration of the species. He spared neither money
nor research in order to attract and unite around him the
three or four French naturalists most celebrated for their
work on eugenics.

"'Marriage is a very barbaric institution,' he often
said. 'I do not attack marriage in its essence, which is
admissible; I only disapprove of the manner in which it
is practiced in Europe. The laws of heredity have been
known for a hundred years, and people have even ended
up timidly broaching the problem of generation, a problem long neglected because of the false modesties and
hypocrisies that surround it, And yet, these new acquisitions of science, which are already applied broadly in
animal breeding, it had scarcely been thought of applying them to our own amelioration.

"'Today, as in the Middle Ages, individuals are still
allowed to interbreed at random, maladies are allowed to
perpetuate, alcoholic propagate their debilitated semen,
defects of all kinds multiply in etiolation, consumption
and misfortune. The observations of Darwin, which have
contributed to the prosperity of the equine and bovine
races, have not influenced the evolution of the human. In

spite of our civilization and our enlightenment, we are inferior to the Greeks, whose ideal was to create children healthy in body and to ally vigor with beauty, What the ancients tried to attain empirically, we can now, thanks to the progress of science, realize reliably, regenerating society.'"

"Those are good theories," agreed Fortier.

"You shall see how Henri the Great applied them. Desirous of leaving all liberty with regard to pleasure, he resolved that feminine beauty, a natural masterpiece, ought to be as communal and inalienable as masterpieces of art. On the other hand, however, he decreed that every citizen would also assume the duties of paternity, by procreating and nourishing two children, if the scientific council of the island judged him worthy, or by adopting two if his constitution was not appropriate to augment, or at least conserve, the virtues of his race. In the month of May every year, the handsome and robust citizens come in turn to spent a fortnight in this palace, where they are maintained and lodged at the expense of the state. They serve as fecundators."

"And the women?"

"The women have the same obligations but the choice is made in another way. Every daughter who reaches her fourteenth year is brought by her parents to my palace. She spends a first night with one of the officers of the guard and a second in my bed. There I make a summary judgment of her physical advantages and her sensibility and fix her destiny in accordance with my impressions. I send her to the Gardens of Pleasure if her beauty surpasses her health and if she is worthy to serve initially for the pleasurable needs of the city. In the contrary case, when she enjoys the vital equilibrium, not exempt from coldness, that the ancients attributed to Diana and Juno, I sent her directly to the Palace of Insemination. But even the beautiful women that I send initially to ornament the Garden of Pleasures must also, after having stayed there for five years, come here in order to pay their tribute to the city."

"That's very ingenious," said Fortier.

"Now," the King went on, "I'm not infallible, and that is why my Council of Ministers checks my judgments. For my Council of Ministers—and you'll recognize another of Henri the Great's sage measures here—is formed exclusively of men of science, who live isolated from the rest of the population. If, in Europe, scientists have failed as ministers and statesmen it's because political responsibilities there require a taste for base flattery and intrigue, and are by that very token in discord with the scientific vocation. In Pamphilia, where all institutions respect and follow nature and where cunning and diplomacy are unnecessary, scientific government prospers and succeeds."

"I thought that the founder of Pamphilia wanted to get away from science and thought."

"So he proscribed them on the island in order that his subjects could live tranquilly. But he nevertheless used them to increase their happiness without their being aware of it, and to edify the future more solidly."

Fortier sketched a gesture of approval.

"Now we'll go inside," the King continued, "But let me beg you, as far as possible, not to address a word to the women we might encounter there. During their sojourn here, we try not to disturb them, and we maintain them in happy thoughts by all means possible. A few works of art offer an easily graspable beauty, a few collections of popular legends, facile music and short walks in the large gardens that extend around the establishment—those are the distractions and accidents of their life. Needless to say, no man can enter here without the permission of the director, since it's evident that all carnal commerce during the time of gestation might compromise the purity of the future fruit."

They went in.

"You see the rooms lined up as far as the eye can see," Henri explained. "The majority of the boarders are resting and those who are not lying on couchettes are enjoying themselves or chatting in the gardens.

First, the King introduced his guest into a large room entirely hung with blue velvet, with delightful paintings on the ceiling taken from the fable of Perseus rescuing Andromeda.

Low frequency electric coils, panels and cathode ray tubes were visible in a corner, separated by curtains and fitted into a scientific cabinet.

"That's the Vestibule of Assortments," said the King. "Every man who enters the establishment is immediately confided to the scientists, who measure his strength with the dynamometer, his structure by means of X-rays and his microbial resistance with the aid of the opsonic indicator, his heredity by seriodiagnostics, the integrity of his organs by auscultation an auxiliary examinations. They also note his cranial capacity, his degree of emotivity and his sensory receptivity. In that way, we have a complete picture that allows a precise estimation of his children's likely attributes, from the viewpoint of health and strength. It is then sufficient to consult the corresponding files of the women to find the complementary female who can compensate for the small lacunae of his constitution, make the best alliance with his qualities and contribute as much as possible to the prosperity of his race. Naturally, there are failed experiments and unexpected results, not to mention that nature still keeps a few secrets. Nevertheless, the success of the system is admirable."

"What about the weak, the defective and the sick?"

"We separate them, sending them to infecund pleasures, only retaining choice individuals for reproduction. In any case, thanks to that long elimination, hygiene, the salubrious climate and the radical abolition of sadness and imaginative exuberance, we have very few defects nowadays. Morbid individuals become extinct for lack of reproduction. Last year, of three hundred males presented for hygienic checking, only seven were rejected."

"That's very good!"

The King went into a smaller room devoid of windows, where the temperature as stifling and lamps with a violet radiance were spreading a kind of mysterious aurora. Pierre Fortier perceived crystal vats filled with small flasks containing cultures. They were lined up around the wall, linked to one another by flexible tubes.

"They're the Seminal Archives," said the King.

Fortier did not understand.

"It's a matter of a scientific innovation little known in Europe, which we have adopted and perfected. You know that Alexis Carrel's discoveries, more than a hundred years ago, already permitted the indefinite conservation of liquids and living tissues. The activity of sperm can also be maintained; there was only one step to take and it has been taken. When a particularly strong and healthy individual furnishes magnificent children we do not content ourselves with the twenty years of his perfect blossoming but keep his precious generative virtues in an unlimited fashion in order to be able to reproduce and multiply his race at will."

"In what manner?"

"By artificial fertilization. It's a very simple and very old method that doesn't necessitate the slightest participation of the male. Last year an exceptionally beautiful woman was injected with the semen of the famous Hercules of the Green Bay, a Pamphilian who remains famous for his corporeal vigor and cheerful temperament. Hercules died thirty-two years ago, and yet his child born three months ago is a splendid baby, well-proportioned and entirely disposed to surpass his father in health. Thus far, in fact, there are two hundred and thirty-two children of all ages belonging to the Hercules of the Green Bay. It is one of the most beautiful races of the island."

"Who takes charge of all those children, then?"

"Those who do not have or are not permitted to have them. Although not everyone is permitted to perpetuate the race, all are obliged, as I told you, to nourish two children and raise them to the age of puberty."

"And women lend themselves to artificial fecundation?"

"It's not them who lend themselves to it; it's obligatory! In any case, they don't seek here a seductive companion that they can easily find in the Gardens of Pleasure, but the one who will give them the most beautiful child. There's a kind of competition in that, which the state also encourages by means of three annual prizes. Those prizes are awarded to the mothers whose children are judged the most becoming and the most perfect."

They traversed a short corridor in which the thick carpet stifled footsteps. They stopped outside a closed door.

"Here we are at the Temple of Conception!" said the King, in a low voice.

He pressed an electric button attached to the wall and a young man wearing spectacles came running. On seeing the King he bowed.

"Is there anyone in the Temple, Doctor?" asked the King.

"No, Sire, you can go in. We were making a couple work half an hour ago but it's finished and the woman is now in the Cabinet of Recollection."

So saying, the doctor opened the door and they went in.

The room was square in form. It was illuminated from above, through the green glass that formed the ceiling and allowed a restful glaucous light to pass through, like that of an aquarium. The temperature was mild and light perfumes spread in the air communicated a heady odor of fruit.

In the middle the bed was visible, in the form of an arch, highly placed and supported by a colonnade of sculpted wood.

"Behold the mysterious nest of conception." said the King. The two individuals chosen to unite first make one another's acquaintance in the parlor. They remain alone there for an entire day in order that they can reach accord. In case of natural antipathy they are assorted differently, for nature inspires secret repulsions that it's necessary to respect without trying to understand them.

"Then, the two paired individuals are brought here for three days in succession for an hour. Every effort is made to ensure that their physical equilibrium is perfect and that no ugly preoccupation obsesses their minds. They are advised to measure themselves in the pleasure and maintain the highest degree of calm compatible with the warmth of the caress.

"After each session the woman is placed on a sumptuous stretcher and transported to the Cabinet of Recollection, where she is left alone for half a day, meditating with her body immobile, according to the old advice of Ambroise Paré.[5]

"The fecundated women are kept under observation thereafter and considered as precious vases in which the gravest of mysteries is being accomplished. They are not permitted to communicate with the rest of the island, to be disturbed by the reception of any news or to look at saddening spectacles. Surrounded by respect and silence, they elaborate the future race, the great and serene citizens who will populate Pamphilia in years to come. In our eyes they form a sacred battalion that bears our hopes, a caste of inspired priestesses weaving the future..."

"What if the embraces remain infecund?" asked Fortier.

"There is a recommencement, in other conditions, changing the couples. But that is rare. As propitious days are chosen and the subjects are healthy and well-constituted, there are few failures."

"Do the father and mother see one another again?"

"That's permissible. Every citizen must, at a given age, take a wife. That does not limit either his pleasures or his liberty, nor does it limit the liberty of the wife. They live united for as long as their interests and tastes resemble one another, and as they are healthy and simple, they are almost always in accord. In spite of the fa-

---

[5] Ambroise Paré (1510-1590) was a barber-surgeon who served several French Kings in that capacity; a great experimenter, investigator and improviser, he was the pioneer of battlefield surgery and forensic pathology.

cility of divorce, which is pronounced on a simple declaration of the married couple, we only record, on average,
six per hundred marriages each year."

"That truly testifies to the great mildness of
Pamphilians!"

"But no! The husband who leaves his wife is
obliged to take another within a fortnight, and, the third
time, it is the Council who chooses for him. As for the
fourth union, it is indissoluble."

"There are, however, poor, peevish and malevolent
citizens?"

"There are asylums for them, where public assis-
tance has enormous capital at its disposal. Life here is
easy and almost gratuitous; the state comes to everyone's aid, pleasure is free. There is scarcely any covetousness or jealousy, since there is no appropriation of
beauty or great differences in social condition."

"But what if a Pamphilian desires another man's
wife?"

"First of all, voluptuous women belong to everyone
until the age of twenty-five. That is, strictly speaking,
the age when they are desirable. They frequent the Gardens of Pleasure where every citizen, with the aid of a
petition, can receive almost immediate satisfaction.

"When, later, they become the companion of a man,
they can still give themselves to another, provided that
they consent to it and declare it to their husband. The
latter cannot oppose it, but has the right to demand from
the man asking for his wife a fixed sum equivalent to
one franc fifty in your money."

"He might refuse, even so!"

"Yes, but then he is declared 'amorous' by the
Council."

"What happens to him in that event?"

"If the woman responds to his passion, they are both transported to the Park of Amour, which you will see tomorrow, and where they live tranquilly, far from everyone else. If the husband alone is amorous, he is isolated in a sanitarium and subjected to an appropriate treatment. He might persist or relapse in spite of that; in that case he incurs a light penalty and then, finally, if he is declared incurable, banished from the island. The legislator thought that, in view of our mores, it is inadmissible that anyone can claim to arrogate the exclusive possession of a woman who does not love him. Such cases seem perverse, and they have been expelled, as contrary to the spirit of the community.

"Does that happen often?"

"I believe that there have been some ten cases since my father's advent. We consider them as European atavisms. In a society conceived like ours, jealousy is nothing but an organic anomaly, an unhealthy phenomenon. Of the ten cases I mentioned, four ceded to medical care and physical exercise."

They emerged from the establishment after the King had congratulated the director for the absolute order that reigned there.

"If your time were not limited," he said to Fortier then, "I would have shown you our school, where the children are raised by gymnasts under a military discipline. They are returned to their parents at the age of twelve, scarcely knowing how to read but healthy and trained in physical exercises. That is what forges the superb iron constitutions and tranquil brains of Pamphilians."

Are children with extraordinary faculties seen on your island?"

"Fortunately, that does not happen often. Talent is sometimes observed, however, and even genius. When it's a matter of petty gifts, we try to attenuate them and to distract the child. If, on the contrary, a truly superior temperament is encountered, it is carefully cultivated, and separately."

"Where?"

"You'll see later. For the moment, we have to go home. My leisure is over and business affairs summon me to the palace urgently."

IV. The Park of Amour

An automobile of an outmoded form was waiting at the perron. The King climbed into it, followed by Pierre Fortier.

"Today we're going to visit the Park of Amour."

"I'm glad," Pierre replied. "I was impatient to see the place that you assign to amour."

"Your curiosity will be satisfied," said the King. "Let's set forth immediately. We have a long way to go, and we'll arrive late. The place where we're going is absolutely isolated at the northern tip of the island, far from any habitation. Access to it is prohibited. The amorous form a little colony, very distinct, within Pamphilia."

"How far away is it from here?"

"Thirty-five kilometers. That does not seem very much, and I've astonished you by affirming that we'll arrive late. But consider that my automobile cannot, in any circumstances, surpass a speed of ten or fifteen kilometers an hour. Otherwise, it would alarm the population terribly. What do you expect, my dear Monsieur Fortier? Certain inventions, above all those contradictory to our old habits, cannot be reconciled with Pamphilian health and equilibrium. The creator determined that humans ought to be slow. That is an innate infirmity, and remedying it requires the denaturation of our organs and our sensibility. I rarely travel by automobile and, in view of the relative smallness of distances, prefer as a means of transportation a mule, a donkey or a horse. By acting in that way I spare the embalmed atmosphere of my island the odor of benzene that truly appears to surprise and poison it.

The vehicle proceeded without the slightest cry of the siren, the chauffeur simply inviting passers-by to move aide, which they did meekly and respectfully.

In that fashion they went past the large school where the children were exercising, and then traversed the Square of Conversation, filled with all sorts of people chatting as they strolled.

As they approached their goal King Henri appeared anxious, as if assailed by somber thoughts.

"I must confess," he finally said, "that I rarely visit the Park of Amour, and only with reluctance."

"Is it so painful for you, then?"

"You will understand my sentiment," the King replied, "on learning that my own daughter Imerina has been imprisoned there for four years. You'll see her. She grew up as joyful as her sisters, and full of vigor and grace. We noticed that she had formed a close friendship with Stello, the great-grandson of Léloux, the actor at the Varietés, who had followed my grandfather to Pamphilia while still young. We believed that it was a matter of a natural desire, a simple carnal convenience. Although my daughters enjoy an exceptional situation, I consented to allow Imerina to link herself with Stello and closed my eyes to her actions.

"Unfortunately, I forgot that a histrionic taste is hereditary in the Bouvallon family. Henri the Great's grandmother had fled Potiou with a fairground strong man, and the wife of the engineer François Bouvallon, the edifier of our fortune, was the mistress of Onésime Tator of the Théâtre Libre. But I had to yield to the evidence and recognize that Stello and Imerina were inseparable. The Princess loved amorously, and abandoned herself body and soul to the young man who adored her. We caught them gazing at one another, trembling when their hands touched, and then becoming as pale as etio-lated grass at moments of separation. Soon, the typical symptoms of the amorous malady—misanthropy, need for isolation, tenacious distraction—became manifest. My daughter refused, weeping, to accompany the son of Admiral Xenius—who is very healthy and whom I have already decorated for tranquility of mind—to the Gardens of Pleasure. There was no more doubt. She loved Stello and was beloved. In spite of her mother's despair and my own dolor, I was obliged to intern them immediately."

"You couldn't keep them at the Palace?"

"I've imposed upon myself as an absolute rule to respect the island's laws and always to set an example to my subjects. The prestige of the crown obliges me to that. By virtue of her violent passion, Princess Imerina had become a danger; it was necessary to remove her from society."

"Why, in sum, do you isolate the amorous thus? It's impossible for me to comprehend."

"The reason seems to me to be evident. Think, first of all, that Henri the Great's legislation is essentially based on the absolute freedom of sexual relations. We are determined that women should never become a cause of dissent and intestinal quarrels in the land. Beauty is the prerogative of all, every pleasure is common to us. It is at that price that we avoid the hatreds, rivalries and tragedies that have bloodied humankind since its origins. Now, amorous passion has exclusivity as an essential characteristic. It is a fervently aristocratic sentiment, contrary to all democratic spirit.

"A woman in love reserves her body jealously and makes it the inviolable tabernacle of a single memory. Isolated in the center of a magic circle, she appears sealed by the ravishing influence of the beloved, and only aspires to remain virtuous. There is even a term in Pamphilian patois, *vanna*, which includes simultaneously the significance of the word amour and the savage idea of taboo. In effect, every amorous woman considers herself as sacred. The idea that another man might touch her, that she might abandon herself in other arms, is insupportable to her.

"In vain, at the beginning of the reign of Henri the Great, people tried to pass beyond, to misunderstand passion, to demand that the amorous support the obligations of all. Suicides ensued. Women preferred to die rather than belong to another man. They would not consent to soil the radiant image they had of their lover."

"That's admirable!"

"Say rather that it's frightful. For that return to virtue destroyed all our notions of equality. The refusals of amorous Pamphilian women would soon have given birth to desperate covetousness, rivalry, crime and violence. By the very fact that she stimulates a desire that she cannot content, the virtuous woman becomes a source of discord, an element of destruction and a social danger. If the amorous had been left at liberty, in very little time the moral equilibrium of Pamphilia would have been perverted."

"You're speaking of amour as a scourge!"

"That is what it is! The Greeks envisaged it as an unhealthy state and their legends depict madly amorous women as veritably possessed, bearing a mysterious and serious wound, lamentable victims of Venus, agitating in dolor and tears. The gods of Olympus sent amour as they sent pestilence or dementia upon those they wanted to punish or purge of their ancestral sins. You will, in any case, have an idea of that when you see the couples imprisoned here. You can tell me then whether or not, brought together and assembled in this way, these individuals, enfevered by passion and arrived at a high intensity of illusion, appear to have turned away from common sense and fallen prey to delirium."

They got down from the automobile and went into the enclosure. The sentinels bowed to the King, who went along a green pathway and reached the center of an immense flowery park.

All around, without any order, stood modest small houses shaded by large tamarisks and ornamented by jasmine and clematis.

A man wearing a red cap came to meet the King and welcome him ceremoniously. He was the director.

"How many couples do you have at present?" asked the King, curtly.

"Twenty-three."

"How many births?"

"Two."

"Are the any invalids?"

"None, except for the Madwoman—but I ought to add that little Arlette, the daughter of the chief of the royal phonographs died of consumption the day before yesterday. That same evening, her lover, young Valentin, committed suicide beside her body."

"I anticipated that!" murmured the King.

As they went into the gardens that extended behind the houses he drew Fortier's attention to the couples strolling there.

"Look at them," he said. "They're not paying attention to anyone else and are not even looking at one another, so sure are they of possessing them. It rarely happens that members of a couple speak to one another. As for my daughter, she describes the delights of her existence by making me understand that she finds herself alone here with Stello."

"You're exaggerating."

"I'm not exaggerating at all. In any case, the director of the establishment, a great scientist, responsible for establishing cases of amour in order to intern them, told me that essential symptom is a sort of general indifference to the things of life, a mental isolation. According to that savant, amour means a neurosis of the memory and the imagination. Those two faculties, normally mobile, stiffen under the effect of the amorous obsession and are fixed upon a unique object. Henceforth, there is only the intense and hallucinating vision of the beloved individual. That absorbs life and immobilizes it to such a degree that time no longer has any purchase upon it."

Two couples emerged from the depths of a pathway.

"There's my daughter," said Henri.

Tenderly, he approached a young woman clad in a violet tunic. She had prominent features, russet hair and a slightly irregular nose, but her eyes were strangely alive, and lit up the face with an indescribable charm. Beside her, holding on to her by one finger, was a young man with lithe limbs and a physiognomy that radiated kindness.

"How are you, Imerina?" asked the King, leaning forward to kiss his daughter on the cheek.

"Very well, Father," she replied. Her extremely soft and musical voice came to brush the person who was listening to it with a kind of caress.

"This is a young Frenchman who is visiting our country and who I've brought with me so that he can see you."

"Be welcome, Monsieur," the young woman said, with the same amenity.

Her eyes posed on Fortier, but the latter had the impression that in reality, she did not see him. The retina could not be sending any image to the woman's brain. It was the same absent gaze as mystics whose vision is forever turned toward interior splendors.

"Are you happy, my daughter?" the King asked.

Imerina looked at her father with astonishment. Eventually, indicating Stello, she replied: "Since you see that he is always beside me!" And she seized her companion's arms avidly.

"But what do you do during these long summer days?" asked the King, darting an intelligent glance toward Fortier.

"What do we do, Stello?" the young woman repeated, addressing her beloved.

"We listen to the birds singing in the woods, and then I pick flowers for Imerina," replied the young man.

"The day before yesterday we saw shooting stars," the woman added. "Afterwards, he talked to me."

"What did he say?"

"That he loved me..."

"But he must tell you that often, Imerina."

"You don't know, then, that it's never the same!" exclaimed the young woman, gravely.

The two visitors drew away.

As they turned a corner of the path, Fortier saw a woman walking with her arms dangling and her gaze fixed.

"That's the Madwoman," the King explained, anticipating his companion's question. "Three years ago she lost her lover to a malign fever. She had cared for him, and when she felt him icy in her arms she fell unconscious in her turn and remained inanimate for hours. Since then her reason has fled, as if out of pity, taking with it the memory of the last tragic moments and leaving the unfortunate woman with the illusion that her friend is still beside her. She senses him; she sees him; she believes that she possesses him. With that proximity, she is tender, sane, generous to everyone, but she does not laugh any more, or smile. One would think that, in spite of her fictitious happiness, a kind of anxiety remains, and that in escaping, her reason has left an obscure disturbance within her, a secret disarray."

Approaching the woman, the King spoke to her.

"How are you, Carminette?"

"We're going to the orchard," she replied. "The sky is beautiful, and he's going to sing me the song that I love."

"What is it?"

Her eyes fixed, she modulated, in a broken but very tender voice:

The moon shines, the moon shines
On the woods, my beloved...

Then she turned to the King. "Do you hear how well he sings!"

When they had quit the Madwoman, Fortier, stirred, asked the King: "In what manner do they live here?"

"They are furnished with everything necessary and left tranquil. Like the birds, they neither delve nor spin."

"And they're treated well?"

"No," the King admitted. "In the time of Henri the Great, great care was lavished on them, they were nourished on the finest dishes and dressed sumptuously. But we noticed that they did not perceive any of it, that all

58

nourishment had the same taste for their palate and that they did not pay any attention to the garments they wore. To tell the truth, they do not know what they are doing. Nevertheless, they continue to be served religiously and with infinite pity. The guardians are told that they are dealing with invalids of election, beings tested divinely by the express will of the Eternal."

Accompanied by Fortier, the King retraced his steps.

The setting sun touched the sea, and the sky was tinted with changing glints of opal. A kind of ineffable melancholy sprang softly from unknown sources, transfiguring things.

And they saw one final couple outlined against the ruddy mystery of the sunset: an old woman who, supporting herself with a stick held in her left hand, was giving her arm to a man curbed and seemingly crushed by the years.

"They're the Victorious Ones," said the King, in an emotional tone.

Going toward them, he held out his hand to the old woman.

"You can walk again, then, Idalie?" he said. "I can see that you're better now."

"Thanks to him, I've recovered," the invalid replied, designating her companion with her eyes, He wanted my cure so much! His desire communicated strength to me."

The man did not speak, staring alternately at the King and his aged companion.

Fortier noticed that the woman did not seem to be as old as the man. Corporeally beautiful, she had a face marked with red patches that spoiled and disfigured her features.

"You still love one another, then?" said Fortier, unable to contain himself.

"Forgive him!" exclaimed the King, shoving his companion away abruptly. "He's a stranger! He doesn't know you."

After having saluted them, he took Fortier's arm again.

"I beg your pardon for my abruptness just how," he said. "I have a soft spot for those two individuals, and I feared that your question might trouble them. If you knew their history you wouldn't ask them such questions. They loved one another when young, in my father's time. Between the two of them they now count more than a hundred and thirty years. Idalie was the younger and she conserved, even recently, admirably beautiful features. Their happiness was absolute and unmixed, for they lived on the exchange of their gazes and the warmth that words of admiration excited in their bodies. Idalie pronounced the prettiest words of amour I know: 'I continue to live incessantly the day when I met him for the first time.'

"The years went by equitably and their amour remained inalterable, when three years ago, the man was afflicted by a disease of the liver from which he only emerged jaundiced and fleshless, a sad phantom of what he had previously been. Then a bitter melancholy invaded him on sensing that he was ugly; old before his time, he feared no longer being worthy of his beloved. 'I can't please you,' he said to her. 'I've conserved nothing of what you were once able to love in me.'

"In vain, Idalie replied that he was still the same for her and that his weakness rendered him, on the contrary, more lovable. He listened to her without believing her, and smiled sadly. Then, seeing that his regret was tenacious and incurable, Idalie slashed her face one day and went to him disfigured, smiling and happy. 'You can no longer be anxious, my love,' she said to him. 'If one of us ought to beg the other for love, it's me.'"

The King fell silent.

They walked in silence while the shadow advanced, and night fell.

Now, Fortier felt that he was trading on sacred ground and that a sovereign virtue emanated from those sublime lunatics, possessors of illusion, victorious over time, raised beyond appearances and destruction.

"There's a disconcerting and fatal power in amour," said the King then. "Nothing can resist it, and that's why we consider that passion to be redoubtable. It fashions intelligence and strength according to its whim; it weaves magical bonds that nothing can break. And around the beings that it visits an aureole of mystery is immediately deployed. Amour is the only emanation known to the divinity."

And as Fortier looked at the King in surprise, he heard him murmur: "God protect us from amour!"

They climbed into the automobile, that set forth with precipitate noises.

King Henri added: "One of the essential characteristics of amour is its creative intensity. Can you imagine that the majority of Pamphilian children who manifest great aptitudes for science, art or philosophy are born to amorous couples?"

"I thought that artists and philosophers didn't have the right to citizenship on your island."

"Indeed, we consider them unnecessary to our happiness and judge their commerce dangerous. But although we exclude them from our life, we want to respect their nature and we don't stifle any of the seeds they produce."

"There are philosophers, poets and artists on the island, then?"

"I've already hinted to you that there were. You'll see them later. They too live apart. I like them and I nourish some esteem for them, for I believe that they're necessary to the divine economy of the world. They think for us, they worry for us, and, attracting all dolor to themselves, they permit us to be happy..."

V. The Gardens of Pleasure

When Fortier crossed the superb porticoes that gave access to the Gardens of Pleasure, the orderliness of the vegetation and the noble amplitude of the perspective evoked in his memory the Tuileries and the Place du Carrousel.

Electric lights, cleverly colored and projected, furrowed the declining twilight and lent I know not what magical and unreal quality to the landscape.

In the distance, a series of harmonious edifices bordered the view, while in the middle of the gardens, chalets surrounded by verdure, rustic altars, jets of water and bushy arbors were perceptible.

"One might think that all Pamphilia had arranged to meet here!" said Fortier, marveling at the flood of young men, women and old men who were coming in, uniformly dressed, their faces respiring contentment.

"That's the reality," said the King. "Once a week, on Thursday, the Lord's Day, almost the entire population comes to spend the day here."

"There's no formality to enter?"

"No formality at all. We only demand that everyone takes a bath beforehand in the vast and sumptuous baths that you saw in the vicinity of the edifice. We also prescribe that they wear the costume of the island, a simple linen tunic and a yellow belt, for it would be ugly and disgraceful to see the oppositions of multicolored costumes in this harmonious enclosure."

"And apart from Thursdays, do the Gardens of Pleasure remain closed?"

"Yes, certainly. Our design is to break and vary the equal tranquility of existence by means of a day of absolute liberty and distraction. You can see over there the edifices that rise up next to the amphitheater. One finds concert halls and dance halls there, galleries of sculpture and painting, and, further away, the retreats where, among the laurels, cherry trees and fountains, couples abandon themselves freely but separately to sensuality.

"Art is mingled with pleasure, then?"

"What is more natural? Everything ought to serve to ornament or ennoble the voluptuous hour. Art and poetry can be considered as manifestations of desire, since singing and dancing, manipulating a pencil or a brush, casting bronze or sculpting marble were, originally, for humans what the deployment of iridescent plumage is for the peacock or song for the nightingale: a warm and delirious appeal to the female. In consequence, we have judged it quite natural that human art should be at the service of lust and that it finds its full expansion therein. Naïve and cheerful singers who do not strive to make Pamphilians think and do not risk saddening them or even stirring their emotions, are invited to come here and recite their ballads, and I also exhibit in appropriate halls all kinds of healthy paintings and sculptures that tend to exalt the beauty of nature and translate the admiration that a beautiful landscape, a fine line or a quivering nudity produces. Finally, it is only in these places that music is permitted, truly admirable to accompany pleasure, but which, in the current of ordinary existence, might trouble the soul and lead us to seek impossible joys."

"I can see in the distance an austere edifice that seems to dominate the others?"

"That's the Great Chapel, consecrated to meditation and prayer. It's open to everyone."

Fortier looked at him in astonishment.

"I imagine that surprises you," the King continued. "On reflection, however, you'll quickly understand that religious emotion accords even more narrowly than artistic emotion with sensuality. Like many philosophers, Henri the Great professed that by means of the carnal act humans are addressing the most fervent and the most pious prayer to their creator. What are we doing, in uniting ourselves with a woman, except complying with the Supreme Will and lending ourselves to its mysterious and divine designs? Is there any other moment of close and delightful communion with august forces, except that of sensual anguish, when, transfigured and demented, we confide our substances to the future? That is why my grandfather, who was an admirer of Renan, repeated continually the words of the Abbess of Jouarre who, at the moment of possession, believed that she was making contact with Heaven and said to her lover: 'You have rendered me more Christian than I was before.'"[6]

After a pause, the King continued: "Henri the Great had, in truth, an elevated idea of sexual intercourse. He wanted Pamphilians to approach it as a portal to the supreme mystery. Before any sensual abandonment, therefore, he demanded that citizens, men or women, already prepared by art and purified by the contemplation of beautiful lines, should also intone a hymn, a kind of action of grace toward the Unknown Being. Furthermore,

---

[6] The line is taken from Ernest Renan's play, *L'Abbesse de Jouarre* (1886), set in the aftermath of the French Revolution; the lead character is fictitious and not one of the many actual Abbesses of the Benedictine convent at Jouarre. Renan was one of Ségur's favorite authors, as illustrated by his careful study of *M. Renan devant l'amour* (1923)

one passes through the Great Chapel and one pauses there, before seeking the retreat propitious to pleasure."

As the King finished speaking, three young women crossed the path, agile and cheerful, deploying a marvelous feline suppleness. As they advanced, their heads touched the illuminated region, and the colors of the electric rainbow played over their backs, mingling, palpitating, reminding Fortier of the delicate iridescences of a butterfly's wing.

"It's a veritable paradise, your gardens!" he exclaimed, admiringly.

"You've just pronounced the word most appropriate to this place, the word that was present in my grandfather's mind when he laid down the statutes of the destinies of this immense edifice. Just as he desired that the Pamphilians did not habitually stray from the positive life, he also insisted that their quotidian tranquility, the placid flow of their lives should be interrupted by exceptional joys, by abrupt flourishings of wellbeing. That's why he wanted these Gardens of Pleasure to be concentrated, and to offer everything that might flatter the senses, and above all, everything appropriate to delight the mind and communicate to it the beautiful intoxication of illusion."

"The conception is grandiose," said Fortier.

"In order better to realize it, my grandfather did not hesitate to depart from the rules of sobriety and sane discipline that habitually regulate Pamphilia. He did not neglect any source of contentment. To complete his Elysian and paradisal creation he added, to the intoxications of sensuality prayer and art, the subtle poisons that furnish ecstasy, hashish and opium. There are private rooms over there in which one finds minuscule perfumed pastilles and softly colored liquids that aid Pamphilians to

66

escape from life and ride the clouds, to amplify the gardens that surround them, to unroll carpets of immensity and multiply their wellbeing."

"That habit must be deadly to the health and the intelligence of your subjects?"

"We've taken our precautions. No Pamphilian has the right to hashish or opium more than one every three months. Outside of this enclosure it's impossible to procure any narcotic, and anyone who obtains any fraudulently is banished from the island. One can only, therefore, savor the supreme juices of the lotus that causes forgetfulness of the present, and whose essential virtue is to multiply sensations a hundredfold, four times a year."

"Why don't the citizens demand those pleasures more frequently?"

"They're sane and simple and temperamentally mild—which is to say that they're docile. They thank the Unknown for what it grants them, and consider it a sin to ask for more. For them, entering into these places after the frugality of their life and the uniformity of their habits is to emerge from the real. Hashish and opium appear to them to be miracles. They believe that it is God, rather than the poison, that grants the reverie. You would astonish them by telling them that there is a narrow connection between the little pastille they are given to take and the rare pleasures with whom they are soon overwhelmed. Habit, thought and abuses have neither worn away nor deflowered them."

"And you come here yourself to participate in their amusements?" Fortier asked.

"Which is to say that my family and I are the first to enjoy them. We never miss a single Lord's festival."

"*Lord*, in this instance, meaning pleasure."

"Not exactly. The Lord is God—except that for a Pamphilian, the word God also signifies Pleasure, Light and the Unknown"

"That confusion seems curious to me."

"It's sustainable. I could defend it as logical. At any rate, belief and prayer are the only capital things. As for the true nature of the divinity in which we believe, that is much less important. It is sufficient that one crystallizes one's aspirations around some object. Père Loyer says that he visited a savage tribe in Africa that worshiped specifically the King of Hearts in a deck of cards. The tribe was evidently idealistic since it succeeded in en-capsulating infinity within a cardboard rectangle."[7]

"I believe that I've heard you say that your beliefs are analogous to those of Occidental people."

"That's correct. Henri the Great judged it easier not to create a new religion wholesale. Such attempts usually turn out badly. He therefore adopted the ancient religions, while purifying them of any moral constraint and setting aside anything radically sad. Our belief is a kind of free Franciscanism, a cheerful adoration of nature. My grandfather tried, above all, to abolish the fear of death. As he found decrepitude repulsive he permitted the suicide of any old man having reached the age of sixty. There's a chamber over there, to the right of the chapel, in which once can put an end to one's life by means of the most improved methods of science. One breathes an

---

[7] A probably-inaccurate and perhaps totally fictitious account of the travels of the Dominican missionary Godefroy Loyer (1660-1715) was posthumously published in 1723, but became far better known when some of its details were reproduced in Antoine-François Prévost's *Histoire générale de voyages* (1747)

atmosphere there composed of essence of violets, hydro-
cyanic acid and chloroform. The person who goes in is
overtaken by a numbness, loses consciousness agreea-
bly, and never recovers it."

"I believe that there are also pagan elements in
Pamphilia," said Fortier. "Princess Monique speaks
about the sun and springs with veneration."

"We are, quite simply, wonderstruck by natural
forces. Tender souls see them as divine manifestations.
Water, the sun and the stars are personified. I don't discourage that tendency. In the present state of our
knowledge it appears to me to be more natural to worship the Sun, the uncontested Lord of seven planets, the
manifest Source of all life, the Cause of our movements
and our sensations, than Yahweh, who was a gross Ori-
ental idol, or Progress, which is an uncertain notion."

"I won't contradict you there. But let me confess to
you that I can't quite grasp what isn't pagan in your religion."

"All the essential things, my dear Monsieur Fortier—primarily and principally the belief in another life, a
Semitic discovery that helps the multitude to support
suffering better. After that, the fear of the Devil…"

"The Devil?"

"Yes. My grandfather carefully conserved—or rather restored—Satan. He left him his age-old attributes
and inspired Pamphilians with a great aversion in his
regard."

"But what is the interest of that superstition?"

"An immense interest. The Devil, for Pamphilians
as for Christians of all times, for Saint Anthony or for
Luther, is the philosopher, the thinker, the logician. Satan is the spirit of finesse. To fear him is, in effect, to
fear controversy, the effort of reflection, all subtlety, all

originality. He is also the supreme artist. In brief, the Devil, for a good Pamphilian, is everything that is opposed to tranquility and tradition; he's the new and the unknown...

"But with your permission, we'll rejoin the Queen and the Princesses, whom I see over there. It's the time when we go to intone the hymn and I ought to be beside my family."

"Is it Henri the Great who composed the hymn?"

"No, he found it in use among the few savages of the island and conserved it out of respect. It's a matter of a simple prayer, very primitive, worth as much as all the rest."

"You don't say it yourself? I thought you were the chief priest of your kingdom?"

"That's true, but since my coronation I've used the pretext of a slight hoarseness and I've left to the Minster of Traditions and Customs the privilege of reciting the hymn. That's Elemir Plato, whom you see over there, isolated, in the middle of the crowd."

"He has a very expressive physiognomy."

"He is, after me, the most important person in the kingdom. Properly speaking, I only have one active minister. After him comes the Council of Scientists, which can only unite under my presidency."

"In spite of his white hair he seems energetic."

"In reality, he has a very mild character. Being the greatest dignitary he lives with the most beautiful woman in the realm."

They had already rejoined the royal family. The two Princesses, affable and radiant, were holding hands and watching the passers-by with the mischief and gazelle-like grace that characterizes young women. The Queen, standing beside Prince François, appeared to dominate her age and revive a brilliant but sage youth.

Round them, the varied crowd fell silent in expectation...

In the midst of the silence, the Minister then intoned the Pamphilian hymn:

"To the one who is born of everything that exists; to the one who gives strength, who gives delight; to the one whose shadow is death and whose shadow is also immortality; to the unknown God, we render thanks...

"To the one who, by his power, is the sole King of the living world and the world that will live; to the one who governs everything and orders everything; to the unknown God, we render thanks...

"To the one of whom the snowy mountains, and the sea, and the distant shores, and the entire extent, and all of time, proclaim the grandeur; to the one who measured the Light, who made the Fire and whose suspended above us the breathable Air; to the unknown God, we render thanks...

"May he not destroy us, not induce us to think, not project us far from our nest; may he accord us health, contentment, enable out enterprises succeed, multiply our pleasures, fortify our inseminations and deign to manifest himself more clearly to our children, without, however, dazzling them! Thus might it be!"

The Minister fell silent.

Then, in a tone less powerful, addressing the people: "Everyone will be able to pray later, at his convenience, in the Great Chapel. For today the King offers a glass of supplementary liquor."

A murmur of approval went up, and then died away.

And the Pamphilians set off in various directions, dispersing.

"We can stroll a little together," proposed the King, hesitantly.

"I beg you to excuse me," said the heir to the crown, but I need to go and join Idalda, the chamberlain's daughter, whom I arranged to meet yesterday.

"As for us, we're already late. We're awaited in the gardens," added the Princesses in their turn.

"You're free, my children," accorded the King. "In addition, the Queen must go too, and I cannot stay away from the public enjoyments any longer. You, Monsieur Fortier, do as you please. You know enough about the place and our mores. Furthermore, the population is mild and knows that you're my guest. You can therefore go anywhere and examine anything. As for women, when they wear a red butterfly on the breast, approach them without hesitation. They belong to the Gardens and are free. You have only to choose. When they do not wear the red butterfly it is necessary to ask them with more reserve whether they want to go with you. If necessary, you can also ask their companion, in the same fashion. It's very easy, as you see."

Pierre Fortier thanked and saluted the King, and then wandered around on his own, at random.

The flow of people carried him away and caused him to go into a room where people were gathered around a table. On looking at it more attentively, he realized that they were playing roulette.

Well, he said to himself, *Henri the Great must have been a client of Monte Carlo.*

He addressed a young man who was quietly placing an ivory disk on the green baize. "What do you win by playing?" he asked him.

The other looked at him and replied: "You must not be from the island."

"No, indeed, I'm a stranger."

"I don't quite understand, Monsieur, what you mean by the word *win*."

"But what is it you're doing here?"

"This is it: when we come in we're given ten white disks. If the number that we play on comes up, our white disk is exchanged for a blue disk."

"And when they're all blue, what will you do with them?"

"I'll return them and go away."

"And that amuses you?"

"Oh, greatly, Monsieur!" said the Pamphilian, blushing.

Pierre marveled. He continued strolling in order to examine the unknown faces, which interested him by virtue of the mild energy that they radiated, and their unpolished and unadorned beauty. As they passed by, the women smiled at him freely, but without profligacy, and their healthy mouths opened as vividly as ripe pomegranates. One divined the delicious flavor that life took on in circulating in their flesh.

As Fortier heard noises and exclamations in proximity to the door of an edifice neighboring the Great Chapel, he went in. A spectacle almost antique in its severity and harmony awaited him there. Young women crowned with ivy were dancing in a circle. The one leading the dance was holding a handkerchief and extending it to the young people who, grouped in the middle of the circle, were accompanying the steps with a cheerful and catchy song.

For some time, Fortier watched that diversion, in which I know not what radiation of adolescence was triumphant.

Each young woman spun around nimbly, raised her foot, tilted her head slightly with a kind of sly provocation, and then offered the handkerchief like a lure, and immediately withdrew. Fortier remembered the easy poses of Greek vases, so gracious and effortless was the spectacle. When a young man was sufficiently adroit to grasp the handkerchief, the young woman gave him her hand and the two of them went out of a door that opened to the Chapel.

"Why are they going out so rapidly?" Fortier asked an old man who was standing to one side.

"They're in haste to embrace one another, and that's only permissible in the gardens, passing via the Chapel," the latter replied.

In the severely ornamented Great Chapel, Fortier was amazed to see faces lost in ecstasy, eyes as soft and velvety as Night and Repose. A young woman who was praying a few feet away from him looked at him and smiled.

Pierre greatly admired the beauty of that slender, lithe body, as if still imprisoned within childlike gaucherie. On examining the unknown woman more carefully he noticed that she was wearing the red butterfly on her breast. He went up to her courageously and said to her:

"Would you care to walk a little way with me?"

"If it's only to walk a little way, I refuse to accompany you."

"What do you desire, then?"

"I'd prefer to go and lie down with you among the flowers in the gardens," the young woman said, while her eyes opened roundly, filled with naivety and natural warmth.

"We shall do as you wish," Pierre Fortier replied.

She gave him her little finger to hold in his hand, according to the Pamphilian custom, and they went away.

"What must I do to obtain you?"

"Nothing," said the young woman, astonished. "As we go through one of the doors giving access to the gardens it's necessary to throw an obol into the box of retired seamstresses, but if you're very poor you can ask to be dispensed of that."

She spoke in a child-like tone full of seduction. Fortier considered the force with which the various expressions of curiosity, astonishment, desire and ignorance succeeded one another on the roses and lilies of that perfectly contoured face.

"You're attached to the Gardens of Pleasure?" he asked her.

"I have been for a month. The King complimented me when I was introduced to him for the Night of Proof. Then he told me that I was destined for sensuality. My mother didn't have that good fortune.

A quiet pride caused the young woman's eyes to sparkle.

"But you seem too young!" said Fortier.

"I'm fifteen, though," she replied, without vanity.

"And what is your name?"

"Rita."

"A very pretty name! What did you do before entering here?"

"Until the age of twelve, like all young girls, I was at school, where we were kept naked, exercising in wrestling, jumping and swimming, as well as sewing and

75

cooking. At twelve our bodies are removed from the sunlight for, approaching puberty, we become liable to awaken desire. Then we return to our parents. We live with them until the time comes for us to go to the King's palace for the examination."

"And what is it that you do here?"

"Here one lives in repose. For two hours a day we contribute to the neatness and the ornamentation of the places, we decorate the edifices with flowers, and we water the hothouses. Then we wait impatiently for the Lord's Day."

"And do young boys enter the Gardens at any age?"

"Oh no. For a boy to be able to enter he has to triumph in competitions of wrestling and jumping."

"It's only the victorious who have access here then?"

"One enters by that sort of selection until the age of eighteen. After that age everyone can enter by right.

Suddenly the girl stopped, in order to make a suggestion. "It's more agreeable to pass through the Palace of Arts before seeking a retreat."

"Let's go to the Palace of Arts."

"We'll go into the hall of singing, if you like. I adore hearing singing. Music is like a caress to me. It numbs me and makes me dream."

Fortier threw a coin into the box at the entrance, watched by a warden, and then crossed the threshold, followed by his friend.

What struck him as soon as the doorway was a vaporous atmosphere perfumed with myrrh and sandalwood. It was gently enervating, like wine.

Soft benches were offered all around and couples were sprawled on them, their eyes half-closed, surrendering to the pleasure of the singing.

The walls were ornamented with paintings. To his surprise, Fortier recognized several excellent copies of European paintings there: Botticelli's *Primavera*, the Florentine cavalcade that, under the name of *The Adoration of the Magi*, constituted the masterpiece of Gentile da Fabriano, and Raphael's *Galatea*, the jewel of the Farnesina.

At the back of the room a blind old man was singing a languorous air that penetrated the soul and was strangely affective.

Holding Rita's hand, Fortier sat down on a bench. Gradually, his senses lightened, the consciousness of his own body left him gently, and a voluptuous torpor began to overwhelm him.

Suddenly, a mouth perfumed with life touched his cheek, and Rita said: "if you like, you can take me to the gardens now."

And she drew him away.

As they went out, Fortier asked: "What is the name of the man who was singing?"

"Lara. He's attached to the court. He was singing the fashionable song which is having so much success at the moment."

"Do you know the song?"

"How could I not know it? Every Pamphilian knows it by heart:

Oh, the bright water, bright water
And blue in the forest!
Oh. the bright water, bright water
And blue in the forest!

"And what comes next?"
"But that's all!" said Rita.

The gardens extended as far as the eye could see and mossy retreats opened everywhere, shady and discreet corners appropriate to stifle all sighs. A languid odor of laurier roses wandered through the air.

Fortier, who could feel Rita's hand burning in his own, wanted to go into the first arbor right away.

"Don't even try," said Rita. "Everything hereabouts is full. It's necessary to go further on."

They advanced, and from every direction a vibration reached their ears, a kind of soft whimpering, composed of very human exaltation that was overflowing there. Every leaf and every flower seemed to be exhaling a voluptuous sigh.

Rita chose a deserted path and went into it. When Pierre was close to her she said to him, in a softly prayerful tone:

"Last Lord's Day, Atmodas, the royal hunter, found the strength within him to keep me in his arms all evening. Try to do as much!"

He promised, charmed by that naked desire, that infantile soul, Then Rita kissed him, and her quivering and replete kiss had the thirst-quenching freshness of a spring...

*

When, that evening, Fortier returned to the King, he told him about his day.

Then, hesitantly, he asked a question.

"Rita was exquisite. Her body had the undulating movement of the sea, and it was unappeased and burning. However, I can't understand why she withdrew to one side at intervals during out intercourse. She appeared to be collecting herself for a few moments, then stammered incomprehensible words, while making vague and seemingly ritual gestures. Knowing your

78

openness of mind, I even dare add that Princess Monique does the same when we're together."

"You didn't ask why?"

"Rita replied that she was averting the 'Advent of the Innocents.' But when I tried to obtain further explanations, she couldn't give me any."

"Yes, it's a kind of exorcism that's practiced with prescribed and regulated movement. You know that outside the Palace of Insemination, it isn't permitted to Pamphilian women to conceive and give birth. After pleasure, every woman respectful of faith and mores is obliged to ward off, with the aid of a prayer and a powder furnished by the Minister of Customs, the Advent of the Innocents. That prevents any prosperity of semen within her. As you can see, everything is regulated with sagacity and every step ordered in Pamphilia."

VI. The Forbidden Enclosure

Pierre Fortier, lying on his back in the middle of a field of anemones, was gazing in blissful somnolence at the sky, where soft and vaporous clouds were floating.

Next to him, Monique, still retaining the lassitude of caresses in her face, was picking primroses and ornamenting her long black hair with them. That hair, undone and loose, covered her back and her hips, communicating to her beauty I know not what wild savor, an ardent impetuosity of a noble animal mane.

Suddenly, a grateful memory appeared to haunt her. She abandoned the flowers and came to put her arms around her companion's waist.

"It's good to be alive and love so many things," she said.

"Do you love as many things as that?"

"But yes. First of all I love you, then my goat Isabelle, Papa and Mama, who yield to all by caprices, the garden, and flowers. I also love fruits, all fruits, even myrtle-berries when they're quite black."

Fortier caressed her. Parting her hair, he drew his hand along her back in order to savor by touch the softness of her skin.

Already, a softness, the annunciation of desire, was breaking his heart tenderly.

In the pathway constellated with roses, however, the King appeared

"I was looking for you," he shouted to Fortier from a distance. "It's time to set out."

"Where are you going today?" asked Monique, curiously, running toward her father,

"We're going to visit the Forbidden Enclosure," the King replied, caressing is daughter's silky hair.

"It's a pity to separate me from Pierre," said Monique.

"Is it necessary for us to separate?" Fortier enquired.

"Women can't enter the Forbidden Enclosure," sighed Monique, sadly.

"Is that true?" asked Fortier, turning to the King.

The latter nodded affirmatively.

"At least we'll see one another again this evening, won't we?" said Monique, still holding her lover's hands.

The King did not give him time to respond. "No, child," he said. "You won't see him until tomorrow." He turned to Fortier. "Plato, my Minister of Traditions and Customs, the most important person on the island after me, has invited us to spend the evening at his house. I permitted myself to accept on your behalf. His companion, the blonde Annela, is the most ravishing woman in the kingdom. One of the amorous recalcitrants whom we banished from the kingdom was her victim. Annela noticed you the day before yesterday in the Gardens of Pleasure. You have only to want it to enter further into her good graces."

"And Plato?"

"Plato is the guardian of the Customs. By virtue of that fact, he can only respect the liberty due to women. He's been informed that his wife distinguishes you and raises no opposition. Nevertheless, you're free to follow your disposition. Instead of staying with Annela you can retire at the end of the evening. That would, however, be the equivalent of an insult to those amiable people."

"I'll refrain from acting thus," replied Fortier, politely.

"It's a great honor to be noticed by Annela," observed Monique, admiringly.

"And you permit me to leave you and remain with her?" queried Pierre, looking at the young woman with astonishment.

"Why not?"

"In fact, you're right," said the young man, sighing. "Until tomorrow, then."

He kissed her and she went away.

The two men went into a long pathway planted with gigantic elms, and walked in silence.

"One might think that we're not leaving the royal gardens," said Pierre, after some time.

"Indeed," said the King. "The Enclosure of Thought, the Forbidden Enclosure to which I'm taking you, is only separated from my own residence by railings. In a sense, it's part of it. Isolated from the rest of the population, the poets, artists and scientists remain my neighbors and are in perpetual communication with me. I consider them as my guests and I furnish their maintenance from my private funds. In exchange, they produce the works of art that ornament the palace and the meeting places, as well as the poetry and melodies that enhance our amusements."

"Are they free in their endeavors?"

"Entirely free. It's permissible for them to follow their inspiration completely, according to their whim. I utilize their productions but I don't command them. Thus, one of our scientists, Stravar, has invented a new substance, Dodo, which, mingled in a small quantity with the air one breathes, provokes a profound sleep. The substance in question is liquid, diffusible like ether, and with a few evaporated grams, one could put an entire city to sleep. You'll understand that, thanks to that means, revolutions of riots become impossible. I have in the cellars of my palace quantities of Dodo capable of stupefying Pamphilia for many months. Think what service such a substance could render the governments of Europe! Stravar, however, wasn't working under my orders. He was simply following his research. He's a great genius."

"Are there many inmates in the Enclosure?"

"There are twenty-four poets and philosophers, twelve artists and twenty-seven scientists. When I succeeded to the throne there were almost twice as many, but the Pamphilian race is becoming increasingly healthy and those anomalies are rare. From time to time, one of the internees loses a part of his talent and his commerce thus becomes inoffensive. Then he's released and mingles with the other Pamphilians."

"You don't permit any communication or alliance between the city and the Enclosure?"

"None. Think about it! The salvation of the island depends on it. That luminous separation was Henri the Great's principal reform. *Let the average and healthy mind not be troubled or led astray by thoughts beyond its capacity, and do not permit the poison of the book, the newspaper, philosophy and science ferment in the poor normal brain.* That was the legislator's instruction. We cannot, not would we want to, stifle thought; let those who are capable of handling that dangerous weapon exercise it, but let them exercise it apart and without spreading the contagion through the unscathed, but which I mean the multitude. 'The misfortunes of the modern world,' my grandfather said, 'originate in the destructive and abstract seeds that are introduced into tranquil mentalities. They are poisoned by them, troubled by them and end up being led astray by them. Revolutions, anarchism and atheism, all the great moral maladies have their source therein.'"

And how did Henri the Great think of making that separation?"

"In that, as well as in the regulation of the passions, he drew his enlightenment from the institutions of antiquity. In Egypt too, the scholars and artists served the throne and the sanctuary exclusively, and were removed from all contact with the population. Their researches augmented the strength and the prestige of the temple and the palace, so public health was safe from them...but here we are at the gate."

"By the way," said Fortier, "why did you affirm before Princess Monique that women cannot enter here?"

"That's true! I forgot to tell you that scientists and poets are obliged to celibacy, to absolute chastity."

"Really?"

"Yes. It's one of my grandfather's wisest and most profound ideas. He thought that, absurd in the clergy, to which Catholicism had introduced it, chastity was necessary to the production of works of art. All literary, artistic or scientific creation is a diminution of sensual forces. That is why the great discoveries, as well as great poetic or plastic conceptions, have been the product of continence. Sensuality and amour are in contradiction and in conflict with artistic activity. Sensual exaltation commences by serving the imaginative labor, but can only end up thwarting it, since it is drawing upon the same sources. Carnal desire ought, therefore, to be stimulated in artists and thinkers but not satisfied, for, to paint, sing or philosophize is to deflect the creative virtues that nature reserves for the continuation of the race. It is in that regard that genius is a monstrosity."

"The inhabitants of the Enclosure are severed from all pleasure, then?"

"On the contrary, we care for them, furnishing them with the finest nutriments, the best wines, all comforts and all luxuries compatible with the deep-seated simplicity of Pamphilia. They are even above the law. They can smoke, converse at length, drink, get drunk, think relentlessly, say anything and do anything. It is only women that are forbidden to them. They would impede their mission. In addition—although this is secondary—we do not want genius to reproduce. The children of great men are usually ill-formed and lamentable. We avoid them."

"So these individuals live without smiles, without amour."

"Let's not exaggerate. For a fortnight every year they have plenary leave. They interrupt their work. Then, all women recognized as sterile enter the Enclosure and stay there joyfully. The rest of the year, the chastity here is absolute."

Then, stopping in front of a small house entirely buried in the verdure and bordered with *agnus castus*. The King continued: "This is where the most inoffensive of my boarders lives. He's a philosopher whose doctrine is so closely in conformity with Pamphilian mores and whose speech is so relaxing that I'm thinking of releasing him. In any case, I permit him to take part in our fêtes from time to time, at which he speaks, and edifies the populations. His aspect is pleasant."

They knocked, and found themselves confronted by a very old and very mild-mannered man. His face was round and his eyes, blue and pale, almost glaucous, seemed to be languishing in an idle dream. A kind of amenable politeness and extreme quietude was expressed in all the gestures and movements of the old man, who first offered chairs to his guests and then addressed the King:

"The infirmities with which the unknown Being has provided me abundantly, are binding me and immobilizing my limbs. I therefore lack the suppleness necessary to welcome you and exercise the duties of hospitality. My heart, however, believe me, still remains benevolent and sincere."

"Ravalo is the glory of our philosophy," said the King to Fortier after having made the introductions. He thinks that ignorance is the only appreciable good in the world. He forbids all knowledge that comes to break the vital rhythm."

"Yes," said the philosopher, "I believe that the true ideal resides in bliss. The natural position of the human being toward his creator ought to be a state of adoration by which God and man attain one another, correspond and are confounded. As for life, it can be considered as an abysm of grace, an endless dream, an illumination. To contemplate nature attentively and to raise oneself up solely by that contemplation to celestial visions: such appears to me to be the veritable goal of existence. Now, knowledge becomes, in that case, the quintessence of evil, since any thought can only interrupt that enchanting dream, that state of delight, the adoring ecstasy that life ought to be."

"The true wisdom therefore resides in ignorance?" asked Fortier.

"Yes," the philosopher replied, "the true wisdom would be to yield entirely to natural suggestions, to be in harmony with flowing waters, blooming flowers, fraternal fire, the birds our elders, living in accordance with the will of the Ignored, who created us of the same substance and for the same ends as the grass of the fields and the celestial clouds."

They bade the old man farewell.

As they went out, Fortier said to the King: "There appears to me, in fact, to be little danger in that man living among the Pamphilians. His philosophy is placid and in accord with the spirit of your legislation."

"Unfortunately," the King replied, "it constitutes an entire body of doctrine. It holds together and is proven—and any opinion that can be developed and proven becomes redoubtable by virtue of that very fact. It fanaticizes."

They walked a short way and found themselves on a path dotted with little square houses decked with verdure, bearing an extraordinary resemblance to Japanese houses. Each one had its back turned to the street and opened toward gardens planted with trees and ornamented with fountains.

"We're still in the philosophers' quarter. We'll go to see Merso, the contemplator of Truth. The others are less interesting.

They went in. Merso was in his garden attending to his cabbages, and watering them with the aid of an immense watering-can that he was waving diligently.

"My guest and friend Pierre Fortier," the King said to him, "would like to have a very elementary and inevitably incomplete idea of your doctrine. I would have given it to him myself, in a few words, but I fear betraying you."

Merso, who was still young and had a slender body, a blond beard and small searching eyes replied that he was do it himself with pleasure. He turned to Fortier.

"My fundamental idea is that verity is an illusion. Our certainties repose upon our ignorance. They change with the progress of our knowledge and are incessantly deformed.

"Consider the sciences. Physics, for example, was supported at the beginning of the twentieth century on a few seemingly unshakable principles. There was the principle of entropy, known as Carnot's principle; the principle of the equality of action and reaction, or Newton's principle; the principle of the conservation of mass, or Lavoisier's principle; the principle of the permanence of energy, or Mayer's principle. Those principles and others formed a sort of scientific Olympus, and Berthelot and Renan thought them capable of replacing all belief, spreading peace over the earth, changing human beings and bestowing wellbeing upon them. They were not only true, but truth itself.

"Now, in the time of Henri Poincaré, a hundred years ago, those principles were shaken. Radium, Brownian motion and a thousand other facts came to contradict them. Today, nothing survives of all that scientific fiction. The physics of the nineteenth century presents to us exactly the same disagreeable image as the astronomy of Ptolemy, which also appeared to summarize the truth of the eleventh century of our era in making the Sun rotate around the Earth. We can therefore say that scientific certainty changes incessantly and is only true for a very restricted lapse of time. That time varies from a few months to a hundred years.

"As for historical verities, they have no duration. They vanish when scarcely born. Of those that were accorded belief in the nineteenth century, not even the memory remains."

"What can we do, then?" asked Fortier.

"I believe, Monsieur, that everyone ought to trust his interior sentiment and only give credit to prejudices. Those do not change; they have an eternal duration that can only come from a deep-seated, real and active virtue. Rather think about the hope of paradise, and belief in the immortality of the soul; our forefathers in the caves adhered to those and we still live on them. While we have changed our cosmological, historical and biological systems a hundred times, those dreams and chimeras always remain the same. In sum, nothing has a chance of permanence except for legends and superstitions. The fable of the shoe of Rhodopis, which was recounted to Egyptian children five thousand years ago to put them to sleep, still serves the same purpose today in Italy.[8] That tale is durable, so I call it true. And I believe in Rhodopis' shoe. Two hundred generations have believed in it, while scarcely four accorded their confidence to Lavoisier's principle of the conservation of mass.

"That is the substance of my philosophy, Monsieur. Amplified and demonstrated it occupies eight octavo volumes, which I am ready to put at your disposal."

Fortier thanked him, without actually accepting that offer, and went out with the King.

"Your philosopher appears to me to exaggerate," he said, when they had drawn away.

---

[8] The story of Rhodopis' shoe, which was stolen by an eagle and dropped in the lap of a king, who then searched for her and married her, recorded by Strabo in the first century B.C., is considered by some folklorists to be an early version of the story known in English as that of Cinderella. Rhodopis was also mentioned by Herodotus in the fifth century B.C., but his account did not include the anecdote about the shoe, which thus appears to have been a later embellishment or transformation, contradicting Merso's argument.

"Who knows? Who knows?" replied Henri, thoughtfully.

They passed under an arch of verdure where clematis was climbing majestically and bending over gracefully.

"Now we're in the scientists' quarter, said the King. We lodge here the electrical physicists, the chemists, the naturalists, the biologists and other specialists that I forget. Unfortunately, I can't introduce you to them.

"Why?" asked Fortier, politely.

"Because they're very excited at the moment. They're confronting one another furiously and hurling insults at one another. I don't know whether you've heard a confused noise like a pack of hounds pursuing a wild boar filtering through your windows in recent days. That, I regret to inform you, was our scientists arguing. They were debating the seat of the soul.

"The Aranists, following the great Aranius—a physiologist of genius who died last year after having forgotten, by virtue of distraction, to eat for twenty days—sustain that the soul resides in the brain. They have, it appears, found a tiny vesicle filed with gas hidden above the fifth ventricle. When punctured, that vesicle makes a rather strange sound like a minuscule fart. After certain very delicate experiments Aranius had demonstrated that the soul is there, in a state of extreme pressure.

"On the other hand, the Pfafferists, following Pfaffer—who is still alive but partially sighed, having lost an eye in a laboratory explosion—say that the soul cannot reside in the brain because they have been able to remove the two hemispheres of several animals without any appearing to suffer considerably therefrom. Although the animals no longer think they continue none-theless to eat, drink, walk and even get fat."

"That's an absurd quarrel."

"It has become envenomed to an unimaginable de-gree. It is reminiscent of what happened in France at the time of Pasteur with regard to spontaneous generation, and what happened even more anciently when the physi-cians of Europe divided into animists and vitalists. Eve-rything repeats. Furthermore, debate is the basis of sci-ence. A university in which people quarrel is a prosper-ous university. The only regrettable fact is that Pfaffer, the other day, let himself go to the extent of making in-considerate use of his teeth and tearing away the ear-lobe of Elda, the present leader of the Aranists."

"That's your entire scientific movement?"

"Not exactly, for there are also scholars who carry out research. The greatest is perhaps The Man who has Replaced the Ether."

"Is that his name?"

"It's his name of glory. In truth he's called Muller. He descends from an old German family. There he is, in fact, at the door of his house. We can go to see him.

In fact, The Man who has Replaced the Ether was taking the air at the door of a flowery maisonette. He had thick eyebrows, a prominent nose and a stoop, as if his research bore him essentially toward the ground.

"This is a stranger who is honoring us with his presence," said the King, amicably, shaking the hand of The Man who had Replaced the Ether.

Fortier asked for a few clarifications.

"My discovery is purely mathematical," said the scientist, mildly. "It can only be enunciated by means of algebraic formulae. I've even renounced publishing it because the tiny printing press in the Enclosure does not have the necessary quantity of characters. In substance, it's sufficient to know that I've definitively replaced the ether. In the last fifty years that element has become impossible. It inconveniences scientists too much.

"You're not unaware that physics, everything is explained by means of the ether. Without the ether, there is no heat, no electricity, no movement. In order to meet the demands of science, however, the ether ended up having contradictory qualities. It was as heavy as lead and yet imponderable enough not to count in gravitation. Its hardness was superior to that of steel while its elasticity left the softness of rubber far behind. Gradually, the ether had surpassed the limit of the incomprehensible. The most serious scientists could not mention it without bursting into laughter, but it was untouchable, because the existence of physics depended on it. Fortunately, I've warded off that danger..."

"What is it that you've done?" asked Fortier, anxiously.

"I've created another hypothetical agent, the *miden*,[9] represented by a formula that changes qualities according to the needs of the scientist. It is sufficient to alter one of the figures, and the electrical miden becomes apt to serve as caloric miden, or caloric miden as mechanical miden. Nothing in physics remains obscure, thanks to miden.

As they separated from the scientist, the King said to Fortier: "I'll spare you the linguists, ethnographers and historians. If you like, we'll pass on to the artists' quarter."

---

[9] The Dutch verb *miden* means "to avoid."

"But what is that large cage filled with human beings that I can see over there?" asked Fortier, stopping in surprise.

"Oh, you've seen them," said the King. "I didn't want to talk to you about them. They're our physicians."

"But why are they locked up?" asked Fortier.

"It's one of Henri the Great's decisions. He decreed that all physicians should call themselves Diaforius, that they should grow a long beard, wear a wig sand blue-tinted spectacles and be locked in a cage. My grandfather exaggerated and was perhaps unjust. In any case, he could scarcely tolerate physicians. The Pamphilians are invited by law to tolerate maladies for as long as they can and only to have recourse to healers in desperate cases. You have, moreover seen at every street corner, alongside the great inscription that counsels Pamphilians to avoid amour, there is another that encourages them to prefer malady to medicine."

"That's too absolute!" said Fortier.

"I agree with you," the King replied, "but I can't go against the received customs."

"Why, in sum, so much intransigence against physicians?"

"It's because of a famous operation to which my grandfather was subjected in Paris when he was still called Bouvallon. He suffered from a bad neurasthenia and, in accordance with the ritual of the epoch, the physicians were determined to remove his appendix—for at the beginning of the twentieth century, appendices were persecuted. He was therefore admitted to hospital, taken to the operating theater and put to sleep. When he woke up, his head was bandaged and he was in terrible pain. The surgeon had carried out a trepanation, evidently mistaking him for someone else. I ought to add that, by chance, that intervention led to a fortunate change and cured him of the neurasthenia. But my grandfather conceived a great resentment against physicians and never forgave them for that error. He therefore demanded firmly that Pamphilia should be preserved so far as possible from that necessary but redoubtable corporation."

They came to an area that was more florid and more cheerful, almost delightful. The birds were singing, the gardens lush, and a murmur of running water and bees was audible.

"This is the Retreat of the Poets," the King explained. "Henri the Great edified it with love and care. It was his intention that it should be welcoming, varied, colorful, restful, light and perfumed. Trees of the most beautiful species, the birds most disposed to sing and the most delicately tinted flowers ornament this abode."

"Do you have many poets?"

"Fourteen. Unfortunately, I can't introduce you to them."

"In fact, it is getting late."

"That's not the reason. They'd sadden you and cause death to enter into your soul. Ten years ago, without anyone knowing why, our poets suddenly became pessimists."

"That's bizarre," said Fortier.

"Nothing, however, is more exact. At the commencement of my reign, poetry was cheerful, gay, tender and sentimental. It married colors with sounds, sought hidden symbols, was exercised in magnifying vegetables, envying insects, cherishing the humble. One great poet sang divinely about 'his brothers the long-eared donkeys' and a poetess had informed us by means of immortal verses of the best way of eating over-ripe raspberries without staining the fingers..."

"That poetry must have been exquisite."

"That, alas, is why is it did not last long. A funereal wind blows now. Antar, who is a great admirer of Japan, sings about suicide and the ineffable joy of hara-kiri. 'The best terrestrial favor is to die and escape from the frightful jail that is the world'—such is the preferred theme of his stanzas."

"That despair must have a reason.

"Naturally, it has one, but it's still necessary to find it. Many opinions are emitted on that matter. The scientists, whose advice I asked, have met in conference to discuss it, but did not succeed in reaching agreement. The explanation of the great Venuta appears probable to me. That chemist claims that Pamphilia's water has contained a greater quantity of calcareous salts for the last ten years, and that the change in its composition coincides with the change in the humor of the poets."

"It's possible."

"Other scientists deny it. Each one interprets the fact according to his own specialty. For Plof, the astronomer, it's the influence of sunspots that provokes that change of humor; for Priela, the naturalist, it's the introduction of cress into the nourishment of the birds that sing in this region."

"What about your artists?"

"There's the same effervescence and anxiety among the artists. All are seeking the novelty that will make their art stand out. The painters want to provoke musical impressions with their pictures, the sculptors clam to be suggesting the sensation of color, and the musicians have invented what they call the perfumed sonata.

"The man who seems to me to be the best endowed at the moment in the painter Voguelot, whose studio we can visit. His paintings are interesting and striking because of their originality.

They approached a small house decorated with pretty enamels in ceramics representing confronted lions. The King rang and went in.

A vastly corpulent and thickly-bearded man came to meet him.

"We'd like to admire your works," said the King. "Monsieur Fortier is French, and knows a great deal about art."

"I only have two paintings in my studio at the moment, but I'll show them to you with an extreme pleasure."

And Voguelot went to bring into the light a large canvas that was masked by a screen.

"This is my best work," he said. "Its title, *At a Trot*, indicates to you that I wanted to give the impression of a moving carriage."

At first, one distinguished a swarm of shades, a merry dance of colors, striking in their violence. The painting was formed of symmetrical squares that were aligned and succeeded one another in perfect order. The carriage manned by a young peasant and pulled by a donkey appeared soft and vaporous in the midst of the incredible clarity of the road and the background of foliage that framed it. By looking at it for a long time one did end up, in fact with a vague impression that it was rolling along.

"That's astonishing," said Fortier. "One might, indeed, think that it was moving."

"It moves well, doesn't it?" suggested Voguelot, satisfied.

"Yes, it rolls. How do you paint, Monsieur Voguelot? I can't quite grasp your method."

"It's very simple. I make use of square of all colors cut out in a kind of sealing wax. Those squares of varying thickness compose a sort of marquetry with an uneven surface. Thus, I can conserve the amplitude of the mosaic in my paintings, accentuate the gleam of the color and, at the same time give a certain impression of relief."

"It's prodigious. And you glue your squares?"

"No, the canvas is steeped in an adherent substance; it's sufficient to place them. My procedure is the perfect coronation of all the innovations that, under the names of pointillism, impressionism and cubism, found so much credit at the beginning of the twentieth century."

Going to the back of his studio, the painter picked up another painting that was resting in obscurity, which depicted a wave beating a pointed rock furiously.

"Do you see the play of the foam?" he asked, admitting his own work. His eyes were sparkling with malice and contentment. His invention was going to his head.

In fact, there was a movement and almost a frisson in the stream of the foam along the ruddy picture.

"Very fine!" said Fortier.

But when they left the studio and the Enclosure, heading for the palace, he confessed to the King: "In sum, Sire, there isn't in the Enclosure the lively originality that reigns in the rest of the isle. Your poetry, your art and your philosophy have delighted and astonished me, but they remind me of Europe. Ultimately, your artists and men of science are plowing the same furrow as ours..."

But the King, who was pursuing an obsession, interrupted his guest.

"I tremble in thinking that these follies, these sophisms, these sterile and unhealthy mind games might spread among my mild Pamphilian population. Art and metaphysical speculation only elevate brains that can support them. Otherwise their action is destructive.

"Look at the poet Antar. In imitation of Goethe in *Werther*, he too declares that suicide is the only conclusion, the only coronation of a passionate torment. He even prescribes it as a determination particularly appropriate to every well-born soul. And notice that such opinions never attain the man who enunciates them. Antar is large, fat and rosy. His muscles are steely, he will have a long life. He is not suffering. Like Goethe, like Schopenhauer, Antar exists with sensuality, avidity and amplitude. But his poetry, his words, would certainly have turned the head of many Pamphilians, and would have devastated our souls.

"Do you know what Henri the Great called the inhabitants of the Enclosure? He called them the disquieters. Philosophers and artists are, in sum, only following their destiny. They are respectable. Their work is the normal product of their nature. But in relation to others they ought to be considered as sowers of dreams and desires, inventors of problems, great provocateurs of moral fever. Agitate your crazy ideas as much as you like in your own brain, but don't communicate them to people who are not equipped to support them. That would be a crime and a dangerous contagion, and it would be the ultimate sin."

The King stopped abruptly.

"Here we are already at Plato's house. We're awaited, and the exceptional illumination shows that an excellent welcome is being reserved for you. We'll certainly have a good evening, which you will then prolong in an enviable fashion."

"One last question," said Fortier, as they went in. "What do you do with all the works of philosophy and poetry, all the paintings and all the bizarre melodies that see the light of day in the Enclosure?"

"I sent them to be printed or exhibit them in Brussels. And I must say that Pamphilian productions have a certain clientele in Europe."

VII. Hell

They walked along a great gallery ornamented by mirrors, which reflected the external colonnade and multiplied the sunlit garden infinitely.

Spring was triumphant over the earth and the air was charged with the perfume of grass and the pollen of flowers.

Obedient to the King's invitation, Fortier recounted the agreeable hours that he had spent entertaining himself voluptuously with the beautiful Annela. And he confessed that the perfect lady had shown herself to be full of novelty and resources throughout the precious and intoxicating time that she had granted him.

"What do you think of her beauty?" the King asked.

"I find it intimidating," the young man replied. "Her husband Plato introduced me to her and I contemplated that proud bearing, that justly proportioned face in which the eyes alone broke the measure by virtue of their excessive grandeur, I was gripped. The voice is musical and lingers gladly on the grave notes. I loved most of all the incessant palpitation of her nostrils, which one might have thought taking flight with pleasure. Later, in intimacy, I knew that Annela is destined particularly to govern everything, to command everything, even the lust of men."

"She's an admirable woman," the King confirmed.

"In the morning she asked me for my ring as a souvenir, and also a written testimony of the satisfying night that I had spent with her. That appeared to me rather curious."

"It's an established custom," said the King.

"What purpose does it serve?"

"Beautiful Pamphilians dream of possessing, at the time of their decease, at least five hundred analogous attestations. By proving in that fashion that they have given perfect happiness to five hundred different men, they acquire the right to be recompensed by a small marble pyramid bearing their name. We erect those pyramids in the Gardens of Pleasure. It's the only kind of immortality that we accord to women."

"With regard to immortality, you haven't explained to me the concept that Pamphilians have of it. How do they imagine the eternal life promised by their religion?"

"You're touching on an obscure subject there, my dear Monsieur Fortier. I've told you that our government offers annual bonuses to those who have constrained themselves not to think about the future life. We enable Pamphilians to hope for a certain immortality of the soul and we assure them that they will attain paradise. Nevertheless, we avoid giving clarifications or precisions relative to that paradise."

"Why?"

"Because it's almost impossible. Unhappy people can easily imagine paradise. Mohammedans conceive of it as a tranquil country in which everyone can eat when he is hungry, drink when he is thirsty and delight himself voluptuously with the bodies of beautiful houris. For Christians, paradise is a luminous country; one does not work there; one listens idly to lovely music made by the angels and enjoys the absence of evils that bliss implies. With regard to Pamphilians, what do you want us to promise them? They enter into Paradise, so to speak, while alive. They enjoy at their discretion, during their terrestrial life, beauty, sunlight, nature, quietude, everything that they desire and everything that they conceive as desirable. They are not hungry, they carry no passions within them, they do not glimpse anything beyond what they can attain. Far from luxury, far from any troubling reading, not living much by imagination, they are unable either to conceive or appreciate the celestial visions that poetic exaltation provoked in the author of the Apocalypse or Dante."

"You're right," said Fortier.

"Paradise is in Pamphilia," the King continued. "Hashish and opium, combined with sexual intercourse, easily offer my subjects the most splendid illusions that their minds can contain."

"Eternal bliss remains, therefore, vague and misty in your country?"

"It floats in an indistinct limbo. What is, on the other hand, precise, clear and entirely graspable for a Pamphilian brain, is Hell."

"You affirm the existence of a Hell?"

"We believe in a terrible Hell. You can make any inhabitant of the island go pale at any time, and you can cause the least fearful woman to faint, simply by pronouncing its name. In any case, it's sufficient to tell you that the prestige attached to the crown and the salutary dread inspired by the royal house is founded on the deeply rooted certainty that our family is in communication with Hell."

"What! The throne of Pamphilia plunges its roots into black domains?"

"Yes, and I'll make haste to give you the explanation. Henri the Great, my glorious ancestor, thought that it is in fear that great dynasties are edified. In order to be loved by his subjects he wanted first of all to be feared. On the other hand, his pacific make-up led him to abhor bloodshed; cruelty was repugnant to him. He therefore

102

conceived the ingenious plan of only inspiring imaginary fear and carefully retaining Hell and its terrifying effects as the exclusive prerogative and privilege of the crown. Once a year, the Day of Dread is celebrated in Pamphilia, by showing the diabolical countries to the people."

"How do you succeed in doing that."

"We simply provide, in subterranean halls beneath this palace, unforgettable visions of Hell. The Day of Dread always coincides with the first day of the year, a day of mourning, since an appreciable proportion of human life is engulfed in annihilation. On that day, the people, through the intermediary of the King, see the abode of the damned rise up before them."

"Is it truly terrible?"

"It's terrifying. You can judge for yourself. In spite of the severe laws that punish with banishment anyone who penetrates into the forbidden halls, I'll make an exception and take you there. The spectacle will finish giving you an accurate idea if my ancestor's wisdom."

Preceding his guest, the King went to open an iron door and then went down a series of narrow and secret stairways.

"I don't want anyone to see us going down here. A kind of panic reigns around these locations, which my grandfather designed under the inspiration of the Mysteries of Egypt and those of Eleusis. Claps of artificial thunder, magnesium lightning and artificial fireworks, combined with sulfurous odors and propitious obscurity—nothing has been neglected in order fully to prepare the popular soul for terrible visions."

He opened a second door. "Here's the hall. You can see that it's immense. A large number of people can take their places here to witness the spectacle."

Fortier noticed that the walls were slightly tilted forwards and covered with black velvet, so that the place presented itself as a gulf of sinister extent.

"What are these visions that cast horror into the soul of Pamphilians?"

"They're cinematographic projections, greatly magnified and skillfully chosen with the design of terrifying. You're going to see a few of the most striking."

In spite of his courage and long habituation to danger, Fortier was anxious. Far from any precise dread, he nevertheless experienced I know not what anguishing and mysterious impatience.

The King disappeared into a corridor, switched off the electric light that had illuminated the subterrain for a few moments, and then switched on a projector.

A slight crackle was produced; a vast milky circle appeared on the back of the hall, and the first image unfurled luminously.

Stupefied, Fortier recognized it. It was the Boulevard des Italiens on a winter day. Under a sky of soot and blood, the opposing streams of traffic, automobiles, carts, trucks and autobuses, mingled and collided, appearing to be confounded in a sinister fashion in a sudden traffic jam. A uniformed policeman, holding his baton, made the menacing gestures of a fallen angel, while coachmen, rising from their seats, carters with revulsed eyes and leather-clad mechanics vociferated heroically, addressing insults to one another. All around, the massive flood of pedestrians, the black human swarm, overflowed the sidewalks, plunging into the mud, or floundered, weaving between the wheels of vehicles. Old men traversed the causeway, darting the circular glances of hunted beasts, women brusquely pulled their pale posterity by the arm, workers hardened and embittered by labor bumped into one another, and heavily made-up thin young women protected their crumpled dresses grimly.

The assemblage of all that was indistinct, mobile, inextricable, and the faces seemed so bleak, and the sadness of the low sky so great, that Fortier shivered.

It must be a holiday, perhaps Mardi Gras, he said to himself.

Then the spectacle changed.

It was now an obscure labyrinth of formless holes, long superimposed trenches, corridors that bestrode black gulfs and open abysms. Here and there a feeble, vacillating lamplight agitated, imperfectly victorious over the thick darkness.

Pierre Fortier recognized a mine.

The workmen were moving about in a dense dust, holding their safety-lamps in their hands and attacking the mineral with their pick-axes. Tall young women with animal expressions, clad in rags, and curbed old men with fleshless faces, accentuated the desolation of the spectacle, which seemed detached from some somber paining by Michelangelo.

Again the projected image changed, and Fortier saw, this time, an infinity of narrow cells, bizarrely but regularly superimposed, in which steel boilers scintillated, where machines succeeded one another or cannons were profiled. Fortier counted seven floors, and everywhere men were tensed in gestures of effort, some hauling on cables, others plunging coal into red gaping furnaces, others maneuvering pumps and pulleys. He understood that it was a vertical section through a giant ironclad, and was surprised to realize how much that assemblage of wood and steel strewn with men recalled and even equaled the ugliness of infernal visions.

On the luminous square, other images followed. There were, by turns: a cabaret in Montmartre where disheveled negresses were sketching the dances of bacchantes in the midst of spectators lit up by malevolent lust; two express trains in the horror of a collision; then a section through a sixteen-story American building; and finally, the smoke and ravages of a naval battle.

Fortier watched with displeasure those familiar scenes, which the influence of Pamphilian quietude had rendered monstrous to him. He was already wishing that they would stop when the lights did, in fact, come on and the King reappeared.

"There are six hundred analogous projections," he said. There are snapshots taken in Paris, London and Berlin, always the corners of sordid streets, mine catastrophes, boiler explosions, the interiors of field hospitals, nocturnal orgies. It's agglomeration, agitation, effort, anemia and misery that characterize our scenes."

"I can understand without difficulty how that impresses the Pamphilians."

"It's sufficient to tell you that regrettable accidents trouble the sessions every year. Men cry out in horror, women lament or faint, old men go away weeping."

"So, Hell is Europe," said Fortier.

"It's a true Hell, and for that reason more effective and terrible. If we addressed ourselves to an artist, he would paint us fantastic scenes populated by red devils with horns and a tail, whereas the documentary images assembled her terrify like a nightmare and communicate at the same time the gripping impression that is appropriate to reality."

"Does that terror inspired in the citizens of Pamphilia really seem to you to be useful, then?"

"First of all, it is not based on a lie. In sum, I am only showing my subjects their future, what awaits them if they depart from our sage laws and imitate the ancestral error of wanting to think, struggle and act. As soon as Pamphilia wants to resemble Europe. Hell will descend upon the island and become a reality."

"That's undeniable."

"I also take advantage of it, of course, to shore up my prestige. Knowing that I retain infernal visions in my palace, the Pamphilians fear me—which is to say that they worship me. I am confounded with the divinity by virtue of my generosity, the liberality with which I grant sensuality and the mild fashion in which I apply justice. That's a great deal. But I'm also confounded with the Devil by the possession of accursed regions. That's sovereign. I can say that, for centuries, Pamphilia will be faithfully attached to our family."

"I wanted, in that regard, to ask you whether the wellbeing in which the Pamphilians dwell is permanently assured."

"What do you mean?"

"You have rich citizens and poor citizens. Don't you fear that wealth will soon be monopolized by a few more intelligent more laborious or more informed families?"

"I don't fear that," the King replied. "My grandfather detested socialism. He judged it appropriate that valor, skill and merit should take precedence over mediocrity. Cities ought, according to him, to imitate nature and be founded on inequality and the ascendency of the strong. Every Pamphilian is therefore free to amass a large fortune by his activity, but he can only bequeath a tenth of his wealth to his heirs. The rest is diverted into the public treasury and serves to assist the poor. The children of the rich must incessantly regain their parents' wealth."

"There's another danger that is, so to speak, fatal The population increases incessantly, while the island's resources are inevitably limited and static. One day or other, the disequilibrium will become catastrophic."

"It will never become catastrophic," the King replied. "We monitor the progress of the population. When there are four thousand inhabitants, Malthusian laws already conceived and prepared will enter into vigor. Births will no longer be able to surpass the number of deaths."

"You have, therefore, anticipated everything in Pamphilia?"

"Everything is forcefully calculated and understood. And that is caused by respect for tradition. We scarcely innovate, we have no mania for the original, we hardly vary. To vary is to die a little, and we want to die as little as possible. My grandfather inculcated in us the worship of ancestors. Everything that has been established by them is sacred to us, we no longer touch it. The evening prayer that every good Pamphilian ought to recite at sunset, when the soul is easily softened and prompt to melancholy, consists of the following words:

"Unknown and immutable Father, be blessed for the good and evil of my day. Determine that the spirit of my family will always live within me and that I do not damage the line of my ancestry by any novelty, in order that I may remain the faithful echo and the living reflection of their thought and their work. So shall it be."

VIII. Reveries on Wellbeing

From the royal balcony modest roofs were visible, enflamed by the sun, long roads shaded by trees, and spacious squares.

Everything was agreeable, everything respired a tranquil *joie de vivre*. Carters were attentively drawing their nonchalant beasts, and fishermen were returning with their full nets, while groups of idlers lingered in the sunlight, chatting.

As he contemplated Pamphilia and the calm sea that caressed its shores amorously, Fortier, penetrated by the classics, evoked certain remote and primitive images dear to his mind: the land of the Phaeacians where the wandering Ulysses landed, and the other where Aeneas reposed after having fulfilled his ultimate destinies.

The King and the stranger gazed at the varied spectacle for a long time without speaking. They were thinking.

Finally, Pierre Fortier was the first to break the silence.

"Your blissful island and everything that you have shown me of its originality, is floating in my mind like a dream. I scarcely dare believe it. When I think that it's a matter of a colony of Europeans, and yet, that I see here regenerated being, blossoming in a natural and simple life, I can't help comparing them with their relatives from whom I separated myself a few days ago, and whose are agitating on the banks of the Seine and elsewhere. You can't easily imagine the contrasts and the differences that that comparison awakens in me."

"I can imagine them," the King replied. "I've thought about that so much myself! You Europeans burn life, while we digest it slowly, going toward death slowly, without engines, without rails, without flying machines. This earth that bears us, we gaze at in a leisurely and friendly fashion. We pay the same attention to the fraternal beings that form the circle of life with us, to the flowers, the winged insects, the flexible fish, and all the marvelous aspects of animal life. Neither vanity nor glory torments us, equal as we all are and free of needs. We fulfill our facile tasks without fever and experience neither great hopes nor great disappointments.

"We have, above all, the natural grace of simple souls, and the facility of granting everything to life that we extract in the absence of passions and the absence of thought. Everything here grows amiably, everything follows its curve, conforms to its destiny, and retains its natural perfume. The young women have the freshness of flowers, the men sing with the birds, and then everyone grow old and dies with neither anguish nor dread."

"What draws the rest of us to degeneration," said Fortier, "is the total inversion of all the essential laws of life. Instead of adapting civilization to them, we strive to force nature, recklessly, to submit to our deviations. At this moment, while we're talking tranquilly, Europeans are running through mud, through soot and through oil, amid the rumble of vehicles, the screech of sirens, the gargle of engines, They're hurrying, severed from the sunlight, alongside smoky walls, attentive to advertisements and insulting posters, dominated by the preoccupation of getting across the intersections unscathed, of catching the autobus, of crossing space and arriving punctually at the futile and sometimes tragic rendezvous that absorb the best part of their lives. The passers-by have swollen eyes and a dull skin.

"Their nights are more laborious than their days, for amour breaks them, corsets squeeze them, dinners weigh them down, thought haunts them, and slumber flees from them. Those who are not undermined by spices, alcohol or vice are undermined by the desire to *arrive*, the desire to bluff, the desire to succeed. Europeans see everything, except for the tomb, and they go forth in an anxious melee, occupied in devouring one another and smiling at one another. Beset by shameful passions, hidden defects, obsessions, neuroses and irresolutions, all of them trot, ride, pedal, fly, march, laugh, seek amusement, make themselves up and love one another, and all of that composes the modern, luminous, merry, monstrous and implacable metropolis."

There was a further silence, and then Fortier went on.

"Here, you have in dying the sentiment of having lived and of reposing after a troll ornamented by work and pleasures. You savor existence like a generous and natural wine. We, on the contrary, gulp it in the guise of adulterated stupefying alcohol."

"There will always be an essential discord between the natural life and civilization," the King replied. "What served as an instrument and implement among primitive people serves today as a weapon of suicide. The original goal of science was to ameliorate life, and the goal of the truth to select and orientate human research. You have made cruel fetishes of them, and sacrifice your health and your wellbeing to them. You support yourselves vaingloriously on a few relative and changeable verities that every novelty and every invention call into question; you exalt certain discoveries that only enlighten the apparent and immobile elements of things, and never cease to quarrel, to fill yourselves with anguish, neglecting all the simple illusions, all the true foundations of wellbeing. You have gone astray in wanting to go far, and you have forgotten that our essential mission was to live in full bloom. What is accessory and exceptional in human being, creative thought, you have made a perpetual haunting, and even amour, a natural pleasure, you have made into an instrument of jealousy, rivalry and hatred."

"If you abolish science, amour and the search for truth completely, though," Fortier objected, "humankind would return to the bestial condition and I wonder if life will then be worth the trouble of living."

"I don't exclude them," Henri replied. "I make them enter their natural furrow and I restore their original proportions. Let science work without troubling the existence of those whose minds cannot support its divine shaking. Let the quest for the truth not deflect human beings far from their proper destiny and falsify their sentiments. Above all, let amour not become incompatible with life and let art be the ornamentation and not the nightmare of existence. Why not think about our body and its physical equilibrium? I request that people care about it, as well the sun, trees, butterflies and divine slumber, that people gaze at the sublime signs that clouds form of the horizon, and the admirable curves of waves. Let life follow the universal rhythm from which it seems to have been deflected, and let the ancient amity, the primitive bond between the flesh and the spirit be reestablished. That, in substance, is the Pamphilian ideal. Do you think it bad?"

"I think it excellent," Fortier replied. "Although my European brain has been primarily seized by its strangeness, my judgment as an impartial thinker approves of its essence. Who would dare to deny that your reforms, judiciously applied, would not extract peoples from the decadence, the tenebrous twilight that lies in wait for them?"

"And the climate is so mild in Pamphilia!

"The fruits so juicy, the gardens so cheerful," added Fortier.

"There's no summer, there's no winter."

"Spring is the season that reigns here."

"One would think that flowerings succeed one another without pause."

"And the women are all beautiful."

"The entire race emerges from the chisel of a sculptor of genius."

"Life flows effortlessly. It seems to smile."

"But in sum, why don't you stay in Pamphilia?" said Henri then, in his most engaging voice. "The women please you and you please them. The scholars have conceived an amity for you, your commerce is pleasant for me, and you can render veritable services by your mechanical knowledge. Remember that nothing obliges you to follow Pamphilian habits right away. You can remain outside the law as much as you please, you can have children and your race will prosper."

Pierre Fortier straightened up in alarm.

"Thank you, Sire, your generosity is extreme. You've already heaped me with gifts and attentions. The last proposal makes my gratitude overflow. Unfortunately, it's impossible."

"What a pity! According to your own confession, you have no family. Nothing, therefore, summons you to return to Paris."

"That's true. However, that artificial and poisoned civilization, possessed by passions and lucre, pleases me more than paradise. Paris is my home; I'm attached to its malodorous asphalt, and it's not without a veritable voluptuousness that I plunge my feet into the Montmartrean mud."

"Why?"

"I can't explain it to you. Perhaps it's because every change is equivalent to a partial death for human eyes. The eternal life that is promised as replete with bliss frightens me when I think about it. What I love is Paris, and the anxious and delicious days that I spend there."

"That's very regrettable," said the King. "I was caressing the project of retaining you here."

"I beg you, on the contrary, to permit me, tomorrow morning, to tear myself away from your generosity. I'm in a hurry to give signs of life to my friends out there."

"I would not want to prevent the continuation of your voyage. Your provision of fuel is already placed next to your airplane. You shall depart tomorrow, since that is your desire."

"I shall take away an imperishable memory of your favors, and all the marvelous and unique things that you've revealed to me. And in that regard, tell me, Sire, how it is that in such a simple, such a voluntarily primitive life, you retain such an open and well-informed mind, such an elevated wisdom? The King of a country returned to nature, you are superior to it, and I would even say a stranger to it, by virtue of your refinement and your intellectual activity."

Without responding, however, and now looking at him with eyes full of sadness, the King shook his hand and drew away.

IX. The Departure

The guards prevented the curious from getting too close, and a detachment of Pamphilian firemen helped Fortier to verify his apparatus and start the engine.

The royal family was there, amiable and cheerful. The Queen had offered the voyager a fine shawl in Pamphilian embroidery, decorated with little ewes and skylarks, while Princess Adelaide had already placed in the airplane a basket full of fruits: medlars, bananas, mangos, red persimmons and cherries, all freshly picked and as suavely colored as autumn leaves. The day before, the hereditary Prince had given Fortier a large amethyst engraved with the name of Pamphilia and depicting a butterfly, the national emblem

Monique had only brought flowers, and she looked at her friend with fond and temporarily melancholy eyes.

Standing with her, Pierre was talking to her. He could not help saying to her: "Will you remember, Monique, the happy nights we spend softly repeating and varying our kisses?"

"Of course I'll remember them!" Monique said, her lips swollen and pouting.

"But you're going to link yourself with other men."

"Naturally. As long as they're as amusing as you!"

"You're forgetful, then, Monique," exclaimed Pierre, sadly. For he desired to leave an indelible mark on the body and senses of his young friend.

Fortunately he understood rapidly the absurdity of such an aspiration. Tears came to his eyes and he tasted the sharp bitterness that seals every departure, the funereal and depressing sensation of separation.

Seeing himself surrounded by all those people who had been unknown to him before and whom destiny had mingled with his life for a few brief moments, he softened.

Then he remembered Ulysses, whom the King of The Phaeacians and the other chiefs had heaped with gifts at the moment of his departure, while the sweet Nausicaa, troubled in her puberty, wished mentally that he was her husband.

Making an effort on himself, Fortier approached Monique again, kissed her, and also kissed her sister, and then the young Prince. He tried to shake the hand of the opulent and beautiful Queen respectfully, but she leaned toward him tenderly and they embraced.

The engine was already turning over, impetuous and rapid.

Finally, the aviator went to the King to bid him farewell.

Henri stopped him.

Turning to the royal family and gazing with fond solicitude at his children he said: "Go. Leave us alone. I have to talk to our friend for a few more moments."

And while they all moved away, the King spoke in a fever, as if determined by an imperious and irresistible resolution.

"Yesterday," he said, "I examined your airplane while the engine was being greased. To my great surprise, I noticed that there is room for two travelers."

"Indeed," Fortier replied, without grasping the significance of the remark. "There's a rear seat. I often take a passenger with me."

"Listen, Monsieur Fortier," said he King, abruptly. "Will you accord that place to me?"

"You want to make a tour, receive your aerial baptism! Nothing easier."

"No, I want to go with you."

"Not possible," said Fortier, utterly amazed

"You can imagine that I've resisted the idea for a long time. I've been struggling with it for three days. Now my resolution is made. Lend me your attention for a few minutes and you'll understand."

Taking the young man aside, he had him sit down on a bench.

"Yesterday, you addressed a few words to me relative to my discernment and the wisdom of my words. You were astonished, not without reason, to see me so open to matters of the mind, so ready to comprehend the most diverse questions. That's precisely my misfortune, and you've put your finger on it. Following the traditions of my predecessors, I felt the duty to keep up to date with news of the civilized world, of active Europe. Alone in Pamphilia, if the scientific colony is excepted, I receive newspapers, journals and books regularly. My father did the same, but by obligation. I like it, and can no longer detach myself from it. For an adventure has happened to me that Henri the Great, in his wisdom, did not anticipate. It is that, although King, I was born with talent.

"Such as you see me, and although I strive ardently to hide it from others, and from myself—I have a true poetic vocation. I write verses. In the beginning, I hoped that those verses were mediocre and that my talent, in conflict with my official functions, would be quickly stifled. But it has been necessary for me to yield to the evidence. As much as, and perhaps more than, the poet Antar, I am endowed with lyricism. On the other hand, I have no lack of imagination, and a great faculty of ab-

117

straction permits me to envisage the highest problems. In brief, I'm a poet philosopher in the genre of Madame Ackermann or Sully Prudhomme."[10]

Pierre Fortier looked at the king, quite alarmed.

"You understand now," Henri went on, "that Paris attracts me and that all my heredities of an old socialite, a former European, are getting the upper hand. I'm only separated from Parisian life by two generations. That's not very much. I experience an unhealthy desire to see that milieu, devoured by intellectual fever, furrowed by light and full of movement, where events occur and are accomplished as rapidly and explosively as fireworks. To live in Paris, to go to the theater, to publish verses, to respire freshly-printed paper, to struggle to inspire amour, to obtain women without them offering themselves to me, to be deceived, to be annoyed by it, to get carried away by it. Oh, what delights! And how I suffer from being deprived of them!"

"Sire," Fortier objected, "You have, however, told me that wellbeing is close to nature. One attains it by dint of simplicity, by digesting life without artifice."

"Alas, I'm not so sure of that," replied the King, silkily. "If I sustained it so ardently before you it was to convince myself more firmly and maintain the illusion. Wellbeing! Do we know, miserable blind men that we are, where to find it? Wellbeing, for everyone, consists

---

[10] Louise-Victorine Ackermann (1813-1890) was a highly rated but far from prolific poet whose masterpiece, *Poésies, premières poesies, poesies philosophiques* (1874), is a heart-felt and desperate protest against human suffering. Sully Prudhomme (1839-1907) set out to write scientific poetry befitting a new era; he won the first Nobel Prize for Literature in 1901.

of fulfilling one's destiny. Henri Bouvallon thought he was achieving his own and that of his companions in disembarking on this distant isle. In reality, he accomplished an action whose consequences he could scarcely foresee. He intervened in the march of the Universe and contradicted its fatalities. For in sum, perhaps our true mission in this world is not to be calm and healthy but to struggle and suffer. To strive, in anguish, dolorously to attain a higher consciousness, tragically to steal the secrets of life—that's another kind of ideal! What, in that case, do questions of ease and apparent felicity matter? What does it matter if we break our nerves, if we burn our life, if we risk madness, malady or decadence? Is it not also necessary for the caterpillar that it dry out, that it suffer, that is denatured, before being able to be reborn as a butterfly? Provided that human beings end up surpassing themselves, finishing victoriously the bold struggle engaged in the beginning by Prometheus, the thief of Celestial Fire; provided that our consciousness is enlarged until it reflects the entire universe; provided that God is finally confounded with humankind and that one of our last descendants succeeds in winning the sublime wager, crossing the highest step of the mysterious ladder that extends humbly from the terrestrial mud and whose summit is lost among the stars..."

Pierre Fortier remained silent and hesitant. Finally, he replied.

"Come on, Sire, I'll take you. Your thirst to see a world that you only know through vague descriptions is very comprehensible to me. The engine is running, we can take our places. Perhaps you'd like to say goodbye to your family beforehand? Are you abdicating?"

"I've left my last will in writing with the Minister of Customs, and indicated that my natural successor is my son. The confidence of the Pamphilians is forever attached to my family. In any case, the island is our domain. That fortifies fidelity. Nothing, therefore, opposes my departure. As for bidding farewell to my family, trying to do so would unmask my project and perhaps cause it to fail."

"It's necessary, in that case, that I climb into the airplane ahead of you," said Pierre Fortier. "There's no wind, the weather is favorable. We'll be in Paris in a matter of hours. My apparatus travels at two hundred kilometers an hour. That's a fine speed!"

He climbed in, and continued: "I think that you'll son regret Pamphilia. Believe me, you're quitting Paradise for Hell. You'll experience nostalgia. The Parisians will be interested in you for twenty-four hours, take a few photographs, request a few interviews, and then forget you. How will you live then? Are you at last taking some money with you?"

"Very little. I desire my treasures to remain the estate of my family. I shall live on the products of my work and my books.

Pierre Fortier looked at him, irritated and marveling. The engine was roaring frightfully. Everything was ready.

"I'm going to climb up!" said the King, moving forward.

But the airplane was already rolling across the grass.

And Pierre Fortier shouted: "I really can't take the responsibility of taking you, Sire. After a few months you'd find yourself in the terrible necessity of selling shoelaces on the boulevards, and as it would be impossible for me to obtain the smallest tobacconist's shop for you, I'd experience eternal remorse."

And Fortier saluted the King with a familiar gesture, for, having been brought to feel sorry for him, he already no longer held him in esteem.

The airplane appeared to become lighter, and then detached itself smoothly from the ground and climbed. In a very short time, it disappeared.

And King Henri returned sadly to his palace.

THE HUMAN PARADISE

To Anatole France

From the bosom of the Unknown, in which you might reside, I would have liked it to be possible for you to cast a glance over the definitive version of *The Human Paradise*.

A large part of this novel is, in a way, yours. I talked to you about it in 1918. I read you a few fragments of it. Some of these pages I wrote, as it were, under your dictation.

But above all, it is the spirit of the book that belongs to you. How many conversations we had on this subject! An enemy of superstition, with scant expectation of supernatural aid, you thought that humans ought only to seek happiness in themselves. Similarly, you desired but dared not hope that peace might be established definitively on earth. In order to abolish war radically, you feared that it would first be necessary to abolish life, which is its first cause. So, far from prescribing, chimerical universal pacifications, necessarily ephemeral and devoid of sincerity, you wished, modestly, that a real consciousness of the bonds that unite individuals in broader respect for life in general might end up becoming an integral part of the mentality of peoples, and permit a true radiation of goodwill and fraternity finally to reach their hearts.

PART ONE: THE PETROLEUM WAR

I

That afternoon in December, at the moment of the communiqué, certain individuals notorious in Parisian society, gathered in the spacious cellar of the novelist Leparfait, were talking sympathetically about the arrival in Marseille of a first Polynesian contingent.

It was in 1949, during the fourth year of the great petroleum war, abruptly declared, which had quickly degenerated into a worldwide conflict.

To tell the truth, for a long time already, the political atmosphere had been manifestly saturated by storms. But the recent consolidation of the financial hegemony of England in the petroleum market had definitively exasperated America, where stock speculation had become the sole national sport and where gigantic and successive Stock Exchange crashes had taken on the allure and regularity of seasonal epidemics.

So, after three years of relative peace—or, rather, small localized wars—Germany, recently fallen into dictatorship and allied with the United States, declared war. She had seized as a pretext an outrage committed on the Polish frontier and had opened hostilities with her habitual abruptness, deafening with the unexpected din of huge cannons the few old diplomats solemnly assembled at The Hague to discuss the prolongation of the pact of the United States of Europe, uneasily concluded six years before.

Then the Latins and the British who, naturally, were not ready for the opening of hostilities, commenced to prepare, without much order but with an admirable abnegation. The war spread like a patch of oil. One after another, the nations of the Orient and those of the Occident joined in the conflict. The totality of the Latins, united with the Anglo-Saxons and the Japanese, opposed the Germans and the Slavs, allies of America. England, Italy and France mobilized their colonies hastily, and then, still being short of men, decided to imitate America by arming the most savage peoples: those of Africa, the Far East and Oceania; the Touaregs, the Abyssinians, the Papuans and the Malays.

As science had progressed in the thirty years that had separated the two conflicts, the improvements relative to mass destruction were multiplied.

A smile of pity came to the lips of old generals when they recalled the primitive methods of 1914. Immense steel machines, governed at a distance by Hertzian waves, running over water and land and through the sky, surged forth everywhere, arrived from all directions, and occupied all the elements, projecting bullets, vaporizing toxins and disengaging asphyxiants. A French engineer had discovered the means of abruptly dissociating the molecules of metals, and German industry, utilizing that neglected invention, had been the first to set its sights on the construction of engines minuscule in their dimensions but which nevertheless provoked cataclysms comparable, as regards the majesty of destruction, to tornadoes and cyclones.

Thus, death was everywhere. It mingled with the respirable air, it descended like a dart from the sky, it ran over the waters. It reared up at every step.

The elements were dislocated, metals exploded and, having gone to ground like moles in subterranean fortresses, the combatants, mobilized *en masse*, launched bombs with frenzy, giving and receiving death blindly. They did not see it coming, like the warriors of old, so surprise was combined with fear in their march and in their actions.

The cities, moreover, suffered no less.

On New Year's Day, exactly a week after the declaration of war, and almost at the same hour, the Parthenon, Brunelleschi's cupola, the Alcazar and Notre Dame were bombarded and destroyed. From then on, living among terrifying explosions, the great centers were progressively buried under rubble, and all was alerts and screams of death in the daily collapse.

Now on that afternoon in December, in Leparfait's cellar, adapted into a drawing room, they were discussing the events. The celebrated novelist, after having papered the subterranean walls of his house in haste, had channeled the electricity and then ornamented the improvised refuge with wood paneling and severe decorations. He received his friends there with delight. For, although he accepted all the other privations of the war, Leparfait could not resign himself to not seeing familiar faces.

"It appears that the English are counting a great deal on their Polynesian troops," said Baronne Lehmann, well-informed on the subject thanks to her amorous relations with her war-godson, Sir John Macperson of the English GHQ—amorous relations that resuscitated the good old days of chivalry and attracted, in these stricken times, the sympathy of everyone.

John Macperson was, in fact, so ugly and disgraceful that could only attribute the Baronne's bizarre infatuation to patriotism and martial enthusiasm. She was "serving" in her manner, said her friends, admiring her for flexing her heart to the interests of alliances, and pardoning her without difficulty for a conquest that excited no envy.

"The Polynesians are incomparable, above all, for mass attacks," replied Colonel Machefer, recently discharged, who had become one of the most influential Occidental press critics. "Their mordancy is admirable. They believe firmly in immortality, and as they have the conviction of fighting for the spirit of Motono—their national god, whom the English show them being persecuted by the Russo-Germans—it's a fête for them to go to death. All they ask is a pipe of opium before the attack. Then, with peacock feathers erected on the pointed edifice of their hair, half their body colored vermilion and the other ceruse, they hurl themselves into combat, invoking their ancestors.

"They must be superb!" cried Madame de Fleurus enthusiastically, who was reputed to love all beautiful bodies indistinctly. Being pious, however, she added: "The only thing that spoils them for me is having read in the newspapers that they depict their god Motono under the aspect of an ostrich. But perhaps it's not true."

"It is, on the contrary, entirely exact," replied André Martigny, who was following the conversation with interest. "It's exact, but of no importance. Representing one's god under the form of an ostrich or that of an old man with a white beard appears to me to be equally arbitrary and gratuitous. The essential thing is to create one with fervor."

Rich and glorious, Martigny, a film director and universally known scenarist, brought a judgment full of common sense to bear upon all things. He had started out as a philosopher but, confronted by the increasing disfavor that had enveloped all speculations outside financial ones, he had redirected himself toward cinematography. There, imagining, designing and performing his own scenarios, he had surpassed the popularity of the most brilliant stars of the old world. But he had not stripped himself of the intelligence or the common sense that had originally borne him toward reflection. Loving life with an immeasurable appetite, he took pleasure in the varied spectacle of the universe.

"I would never have thought that the imperialists of Germany, the communists of Russia, the modernized Turkish pachas and the American bankers would unite to declare war at a moment when we're so unprepared!" exclaimed Jules Léry, an old man with fine and emaciated features. Having not spoken until then, he wanted to make his contribution to the conversation.

"That you'd never thought that anyone would declare war on us again appears quite natural to me," replied Martigny, who had been his friend since childhood. "Your métier as a paleographer, although it doesn't give you much help in living, at least isolates you from the present. What I can't understand is that the governments of the Anglo-Latin entente, knowing about the financial crashes in America and the formidable preparations of the Germans and the Russians, were able to think like you and remain tranquil. They were not sufficiently suspicious of the petroleum that inflames nations. They're not unaware, however, that in 1914 Austria had already unleashed a terrible war whose initial cause was the covetousness of Serbia's oil wells."

"The immediate fault of this new war," said Colonel Machefer, "is incumbent on our fathers, who laid down their arms before having destroyed Germany completely. Having seen it constituted as a republic, they believed its sincerity. And now its brutal force, enfevered by an ambitious dictatorship, is taking us once again to the brink of the abyss. Imperialism causes the rebirth of militarism."

In a conciliatory fashion, Martigny replied that the war would have broken out anyway.

"The production of gold," he went on, "wasn't sufficient for the appetites of an increasingly costly civilization and its demand for wellbeing. The precious metal is disputed, and from time to time a great quantity of it is burned in explosives in order to snatch what remains to others, or at least to make all of it circulate more rapidly from hand to hand."

But Machefer, who was discontented to have been discharged by the government, started explaining obligingly the weakness of the socialist republics of England and France.

"With doesn't alter the fact," Leparfait objected, "that after the initial buckling, the Anglo-Latins are in the process of winning."

"There's a great deal to say about that, Leparfait," Martigny remarked. "If the Anglo-Latins are on the road to victory after four years of war it's precisely because, at the beginning of hostilities, while apparently retaining the same regime, they virilized it and orientated it toward a sage absolutism, with a military police, a state of siege and censorship, especially with a government that, in the admirable expression of President Fargot 'mounted guard on the Allies' morale.' Naturally courageous and intelligent, easily mastering events when they put their mind to it, the Latins understands that the time for antimilitarist and communist pleasantries ceased on the day of mobilization. That is why you see that, following the example of England, not republican for very long and governed, like us, by socialists, the old continent allowed itself to be led energetically, knowing that that was the price of success."

"You're right," Leparfait agreed. "In times of war, whatever color the republics are, they scarcely differ from monarchies."

"Although I'm not complaining about that, I must, however, affirm that they're unfortunately a little different, by virtue of their lack of prestige," Martigny replied. "The republican regime in general presupposes a solidly established civilization and, by virtue of that very fact, a sincere, immutable peace. It hates inequality and stands up jealously against elites. It loves to break aureoles. Essentially insubordinate, it mocks the great and even envelops them in ridicule. Moreover, that works marvelously during the calm—but when the tempest shakes the nations, people recognize with consternation that it's personal prestige, the religion of respect and the supremacy of heroism or genius that are the true sinews of any war.

"Whether they're fighting for God, for the fatherland or for petroleum, men like to believe that they're being led by someone who surpasses them. They demanded to be fanaticized, to experience respect, to have the illusion that wings beat on the shoulders of leaders. You've read in the newspapers recently that our Japanese allies, in order to honor the nominal birthday of their Mikado worthily, captured the city of San Francisco on the day of the anniversary, to which they had been laying siege in vain for four months, sacrificing themselves in thousands. That's because the Mikado continues to be the sacred symbol of the consciousness and grandeur of Japan. He's the object of a cult, his origins are celestial. The names of his ancestors are mingled with all the splendors of the country. So, to die for the Mikado is a religious and patriotic act, and the Nipponese don't spare their blood in order to offer him a city on the day of his anniversary. Do you think that our troops would have the superstitious desire to do as much on Saint Sylvester's Day, the nominal fête of Sylvestre Dusol, the President of our Republic—who, personally, is worth far more than the Mikado?"

"Would you like to change the regime, then?" Léry interrogated.

"May God preserve me from that! My spine would support a dictatorship poorly, and I believe that one can never pay too much for divine liberty, whatever price is put on it. But I'd like the republic always to be, as it becomes in time of war, a republic conscious of its continuity, respectful of an ideal, a governed republic, if possible."

"My God! When will this frightful war end?" cried the Comtesse de Fleurus, looking at Martigny with supplicant eyes.

"Oh, the indispensable, liturgical, naïve question," Martigny replied. "For four years we've been addressing it to our contemporaries a thousand times a day. But don't interrogate me on that subject, Madame. Rather interrogate our friend Leparfait, who gladly draws up horoscopes and who can respond to you by means of his occult illumination. What can I say to you, with the aid of my poor logic, which sees no further than the tip of its nose? To tell the truth, I can't imagine the end of this slaughter. In the 1914 war, the New World disembarked among us to terminate the war and arrange for us, to the ruination of everyone, a haggard and starveling peace. Now, the conflagration no longer has limits, and it will be necessary for half the world to be destroyed before ceding to the other half. Nevertheless, we'll see…"

Everyone got up. A few guests took their antitoxic masks from their pockets and placed them over their faces. Others, bolder, got ready to confront the street without protection, trusting in the antiasphyxiant kiosks set up at the intersections, ready to give shelter to the public in case of an alert.

Accompanied by his friend Léry, Martigny climbed the stairs and went outside, under the sky traversed in all directions, as if obscured, by airships.

II

Martigny went to a little café near the Gare de l'Est where his son-in-law, Brigadier Maurice Planet, who was on leave, had arranged to meet him. Since his departure for the war, it was the first time that Planet had returned to Paris—for, having need of men, soldiers were rarely allowed to leave the front.

Maurice had spent with Antoinette, his wife, two weeks that had seemed shorter than two days. Now he was about to go back out, where further attacks were in preparation and where Death was deploying its wings more broadly than ever.

Martigny had difficulty finding the young man in the midst of the tobacco smoke and exhalations of leather and indecency that clouded the crowded hall. When he finally perceived him in a corner he had once again the same sentiment of obscure alarm that his son-in-law had caused him two weeks before on his arrival. It was the expression on the soldier's face that frightened Martigny and filled his heart with anguish.

However, scarcely eighteen months had gone by since the call-up of his class had snatched Maurice from his newlywed's bed. The young man, still beardless, had departed with enthusiasm, like all those of his age. The approach of danger seemed to have excited all that was proudest and noblest in him.

Martigny remembered that, in spite of the dolorous separation from his wife—married shortly before that departure, the coronation of a long and reciprocal juvenile amour—there had been something resembling a radiation, a fresh outburst of living force, in Maurice's eyes.

What a difference with his face now that war had fashioned it: a face hastily matured, from which all trace of youth had been effaced, a thin, obscured face whose hollows were full of darkness.

"Sit down, Father," said the soldier, in his voice, grave henceforth, moving sideways to make room for Martigny. Then, darting a glance around the noisy room overflowing with uniforms, whose atmosphere was unbreathable, he changed his mind. "Let's go up to the first floor. My train doesn't leave for two hours. I'd like is to talk for a while, and one can't make oneself heard in here."

After they were installed in the almost deserted room on the first floor, Maurice fixed his eyes on his father-in-law with a haggard tenderness.

"If you knew what a foolish pleasure I experience in seeing you again!"

His voice was soft, impregnated with affection and suffering. Martigny was moved by it. He was aware of the admiration doubled with fervor that Maurice had always nurtured in his regard. He responded to it, loving him as much as if he had been the son of his blood.

"You didn't want to steal anything from us, from Antoinette and me," the young man went on. "You doubtless said to yourself that the days we had to spend together were meanly counted, and you disappeared discreetly, without thinking that I love you too. I love you and revere you even more than my parents, whom I've lost. I even think that it's admiration for you, born first in my heart, that subsequently became love for Antoinette. Knowing that she was your daughter made me cherish her as soon as I saw her; and what I love most in her is what resembles you."

Gazing at Martigny with a somber sadness, he drew closer to him. "I've just left her, Papa, and soon I'll be leaving you. Before her I was able to hold firm and not show my distress. That broke me. With you, thank God, it's different. There's no necessity to pretend. One can say everything, since you can understand everything."

And, in a low, strangled, whispering voice, the voice of a child, the soldier added: "It's finished. I won't come back again from out there. I'm seeing both of you for the last time, and my heart is breaking when I think about everything that Antoinette has suffered and will still suffer. I've been her misfortune, me, who wanted to consecrate my life to her. Now, it's finished...finished!"

Upset, Martigny seized the soldier's hands and squeezed them.

"Why are you saying such horrible things, Maurice? Don't you know that you *have to* come back, or Antoinette will die as well. I would never have thought that the madness out there would discourage you to the point of making you doubt your chances and veiling yourself in advance with the mourning of a future you don't know. Rather imitate me, who hasn't lost confidence. I'm sure that you'll come back. It's necessary for this Hell to finish, and it will finish. On the day when you rediscover your hearth and your happiness, these horrible ordeals will be forgotten, like a bad dream.

Maurice allowed Martigny to talk. Then, when the latter fell silent, he looked him sadly in the eyes and said to him: "Why, Father, are you trying to console me, and encourage me? Of course I don't know the future and I don't care to make prophecies. One day, as you say, the war will end, and there will be some who come back..."

He interrupted himself momentarily, and then went on in a resolute, rapid, decisive voice: "Such as I've become, I can't recover my happiness. That's why I'm telling you that I'll remain out there. I've decided to get myself killed in order not to return."

Martigny's hands trembled, and clutched the soldier's more spasmodically. Then the latter, seeing that the old man was about to protest again, rebelled: "No, Papa," he said, "let me speak. It's necessary that I open my heart to someone. Instead of making reproaches, look at me. What's the point, though? At the first glance you cast at me the other day, I divined that the sight of me frightened you. You didn't recognize me. Tell yourself, however, that the alteration in my features is nothing compared to what has become of my poor mind, my unfortunate conscience. Certainly, I continue to call myself Maurice Planet, as on the day I left. But nothing remains in me of the man I was. My past, my dignity and my pride have all been expelled by another, by a beast that now inhabits my body."

He stopped, and wiped away the sweat that was pearling on his brow.

"And it's even worse than that. If I'd become a beast I'd have been able to continue living, living a new animal life. Unfortunately, the old man is incessantly knocking on the door of the dwelling from which he's been cast out. The former man, banished, wandering, unappeased, and who remembers, is still there. And that's frightful."

"I know, I fought in the other war myself, and I went through that," said Martigny, gripping the young man's hand, which he was holding in his own, ardently. Then, looking at him tenderly: "But believe me, one forgets quickly. Soon, a new life will commence for you..."

"A life? What life?" exclaimed the soldier, bitterly. "Before the war, if one lived, it was because of an ideal, or at least the remains of an ideal. Then, people were animated by an omnipotent religious ferment or a civic ferment. It fortified their moral armor, became the light of their conscience, their pivot, their root and their guide. One lived on that which enables life: personal dignity, the sacred respect for another, an effort of goodwill, of humanity.

"The war has swept all that away. I don't know whether it's particular to me or whether the same thing happens to all the others, but in any case, I no longer have anything, and I despise myself for being dispossessed like that, without any illusion about myself, devoid of faith, devoid of hope—as much as to say devoid of a soul."

And while Martigny listened fearfully, reviving his own memories, Maurice went on: "The impetus that enabled me to depart with joy, I've lost. I believed that the war was an exaltation and a glory. It must have been, once. Now, it's no longer anything but a human debasement. We're killing too much, we're doing abominable work out there, and furthermore, it's no one's fault. How can one do otherwise? There's so much enemy flesh that it's necessary to kill, and to keep killing, if one wants it ever to end. The other ferocious beasts on the opposite side throw asphyxiants into our trenches, sowing microbes and poisons as if for mice or other vermin. We repay them in the same coin.

"And if you knew how young we are, on both sides, and how difficult it is for us all to die! It's an atrocious task, to finish off these who are on their way out. In the ardor of battle, while you're defending yourself and hurling grenades, it goes on and on. You fight, you massa-

138

cre, in a fever. But it's the agony of the dying that's frightful, that last breath that doesn't escape before having become fraternal. At a given moment, the one who's dying ceases to be German, Russian or French. Before being reduced to something unnamable, he's a child without a fatherland, without a race—he's yourself, the man you've killed!

"And every one of them, it's said, carries away something of your humanity as he goes. When, after having done that, from morning until evening, one comes back, nothing remains in the human being but instinct. One would think that centuries of history and progress, everything that our forefathers have done, is lying on the ground with the dying, and will putrefy with the cadavers."

Then, drawing Martigny toward him spasmodically, the soldier started speaking in an anguished voice, in a nightmare.

"But the most horrible thing is the bestial rage that the fine work, once accomplished, ends up by vomiting over us as if to punish us. Know this, Father, after two years in the trenches, we're no longer anything out there but hunger and fear. Having become wild beasts again, we begin to dread the loss of that miserable life, even though it horrifies us. Yes, we're all shaken by the abject dance of the entrails, the continual little death that the terror of dying gives you. That must appear impossible and monstrous to you others, who live a long way from the front. You don't suspect that the greatest death of this war has been that of courage. It's finished, the fine intoxication that once impelled the brave in battles and made the intrepid warrior lift his head up high, who, once having consented mentally to the sacrifice of his life, flies toward death and bullets, defying the enemy.

"It was upright, dominating the earth, on their chargers, respiring the powder, that they were courageous, the old combatants—and perhaps you too, in the 1914 was. We were the same in our first attacks, leaping out of the trenches, going to bestride the bayonets and, launching grenades and defying the enemy to his face.

"But eventually, our joyful courage drowned in the excremental mud of the trenches, gradually undermined by the rain, gnawed by the rats, corroded by hunger, and then it abruptly sank, one day or another, under the apocalyptic vomit of a thousand craters that, in a crash of cymbals, a demonic jazz, shook the entrails of the planet and projected into the heavens, in a single firework, clods of earth, tree-trunks, dismembered cadavers, croaks of agony and cries of 'Maman!'"

The soldier seized a glass of alcohol placed before him, swallowed the contents, and then went on:

"I can remember clearly what I lived through, my first fit of cowardly terror, at the beginning of last winter, at Soissons, after a bayonet charge in which I plied my weapon until I felt cramps in my arms. Without having had time to take a moment's rest, still soaked in blood, we were buried in the trenches again.

"Like so many other times before, attackers as we were, we were about to be attacked. From one day to the next the offensive changed camps. It was obvious that the enemy was planning something rude and unexpected, and against which it was no longer a matter of holding firm.

"How can I describe to you what I experienced then?

"It was the end of November. For three days the rain had been falling uninterruptedly, and it was worse than the extraordinary interrogation of the Middle Ages, that demoralizing water torture, in the trenches.

"Against that, there was no remedy, and no refuge. Slow and invasive, mingling patiently with the soil, thinning it, causing it to subside, it turned it into mud, and of us, our clothes and our boots, it made a single fugitive, plastic, cold substance in which we lived, ate and defecated.

"The filthiness of the soil, the stink of the corpses and the glue of the decomposed leaves seemed gradually to pass into the circulation of that soft mixture, the insipid odor of which we were wallowing, into which we sank at every footfall as if into a trap, and where one often left one's footwear as one marched. All our efforts tended to protect our heads, but the water oozed, and poured, finding the means to attain the depths of the soil, tracking us like a cunning beasts, sliding like a snake into the tunnels, which it infested, into the immense network of putrefaction, of the exhalations of the dead and the living, in which one felt oneself dissolving.

"So long as some resistance remained to us, that could still go on; but, malnourished, broken by the cold and privations, where could strength be found henceforth? The time came when the moral dyke gave way. That which had mounted opposition on the first day became bleak resignation on the second. One wearied of living in garments soaked by mud, in the fetid moisture that penetrated our bread, which infiltrated our pores, paralyzed our gestures, muddied our thoughts.

"Progressively, a heavy indolence overwhelmed us. We hesitated to change position, since there was the same streaming everywhere, the same ocher paste, as ductile as disintegrated rubber, the same impossibility of remaining oneself, of insolating oneself, of not being an integral part of that viscous universe. Then, reinforcements came to join the water to break our morale definitively. That was the rats; they had already visited us, but suddenly, with the installation of the rain, they pullulated. Their muzzles, their thin feet, shadowed and animated the liquid surfaces, and in order to escape the more terrible threat of the water, they hurled themselves madly against the humans.

"Oh, the supreme disgust experienced for the frictions, the nibblings, which spared neither nourishment not vestments, which prevented our sleep and of which, nevertheless, we dreamed. How many nightmares I had about rats, because of the omnipresence of that frightful animal, rendered malevolent by hunger, which I was forced to kill in order to free myself! The crushed heads of rats, bellies opened upon thin, lividly pink intestines, those infimal hideous and squealing deaths in which pain was nevertheless nested, how all of that beats time to my memories of Hell!

"And it's in those circumstances and among those demoralizing scourges that the bombardment was unleashed. It certainly wasn't the first time that I heard the explosion of airborne shells and the thunder of supercannons. I knew already to beware of projectiles, distinguishing the drone of large, distant artillery, the dull sound of mines, the splashing burst of gas-shells, and then the perpetual slicing of seconds by the terrible scythes coming from the air, crawling over the ground, laboring everywhere with their rhythmic tick-tock.

"But that evening, after the sinister sprinkling and the range-finding of rockets that had been suspended, multicolored, over the horizon, an orgy of destruction commenced of which I could never have imagined the extent or the grandeur.

"A double explosion of mines, of which we were the umbilicus, opened the horror, and I suddenly saw, after a kind of immense crack that knocked me down, the sky spitting trees, fragments of earth, the debris of walls, while ear-splitting, gut-wrenching screams rose up everywhere. Then, suddenly, in a kind of transformation of being, everything that was not fear left me, and I was no more than a hunted beast, maddened by panic.

"A tremor of all the limbs took possession of me, and since then, every attack brigs it back to me, the fear of dying, the mad anguish that inhibits all movement in me at times, which turns my skin blue and demolished my consciousness, Hating life and dreading death, I stay there, panic-stricken, shitting myself, governed in spite of everything by animal fear by that bitch of a life, which sounds the tocsin and clings to my fibers."

The young man wiped his brow again. He was utterly pale, and there was a kind of savage flame dancing strangely in his pupils.

Martigny pulled away from the frenetic grip that was clutching his wrist, so emotional was he himself. Memories and visions analogous to those Maurice was evoking terrorized him, surging forth like phantoms from the depths of his own past. His own war, the old war, came back to haunt him.

"But you're making progress now, though," he stammered, in order to break the nightmare. "You're in the process of winning."

"Yes, we have the upper hand—which means that, for the moment, we're exploding more mines than them and they're more exhausted than we are. As for a victory, there is none, in this war, or at least, one doesn't have the sensation that there is. One changes position, like the pawns on a chessboard. That's all."

After which, closing his eyes, he went on: "Forgive my weakness, Papa. It was absolutely necessary for me to confess all that to someone, that I say what human-kind is becoming, what disaster is swallowing humans up by means of war as it's practiced today. I needed to show the horrible ulcer that's gnawing my soul. It's also necessary that you know the truth when, tomorrow, you learn that I died a hero."

"No, Maurice!" cried Martigny. "It's necessary not to repeat that you're going to get yourself killed! Suffer for Antoinette, if you no longer have the strength to suffer for yourself."

"Do you want me, then, to bring back to her the pretty memory of all that I've accomplished?" the soldier interrogated, grimacing a bitter smile. "Do you want me to lie beside her with the bloody burden that weighs upon me? And what if I make her a child, Papa, if my seed of Cain grows within her? Do you think that I have the right to put into the world a being that will perpetu-ate what was born in my consciousness eighteen months ago?"

The soldier got up, and then slumped back.

"After all, who knows? Perhaps I'm wrong. Why, after all, should there be a difference between men and wolves? You lived, you others, after the 1914 war, and had children. We'll imitate you. And in any case, per-haps it's by virtue of a last boastful cowardice that I af-firm that I'll have the courage to take the ten steps that separate my from the opposite trench in order to receive a grenade. Rather tell Antoinette to send me the alcohol she promised me. That will help me to forget, a little, to brutalize myself and to come back. But then, what hor-ror, Papa, what horror!"

144

III

After arriving home late at night, having put the poor human rag that had unveiled his soul to him on the train, Martigny could not sleep.

Memories of the 1914 war flooded back, shreds of his own Hell, and then other shreds of the life after the war, of his bloody and terrible adaptation to the peace and the forgetfulness.

Isn't Maurice right, in fact, he thought. *He's right to refuse to come back and to wish for death. How will Europe and humankind be able, once again, to bury their war-torn soul? How can they succeed in passing a sponge over what was? And what storms will follow, in the future peace? Would it not be better to die, after what one has suffered, and done?*

Irresistibly, Martigny went to take from his desk drawer a secret notebook that he had once written for himself. He had consigned to it the troubles of his conscience, the miseries and the darkness of his life, after 1914.

He opened it and scanned the preliminary pages that, at a few decades' distance, appeared to respond to Maurice's cries as an echo responds to a sound.

He read:

I'm setting forth to draft these notes ten years after the war. It's a long way from us, the war, in the year 1929.

We are now witnessing the rush toward pleasures, the apogee of dancing, the triumph of money.

Europe is renewed in its appearances and also in its mores. Gold, it is true, is no longer seen, but banknotes are raining down and flowing everywhere. And everywhere the folly of jazz is deploying, while women—the invariably precious commodity—tempt more overtly with their gaze, promise more easily the embrace of their arms, allow all-comers to divine the unknown surprises of the profundities of their bodies.

In Paris, London and Berlin, the mingled races are enriching themselves and amusing themselves, whirling in the new sumptuous, syncopated, rapid life—the hard life, opulent, insouciant and liberated.

Enjoy!

It is running toward enjoyment, the world, toward sophisticated dishes, costly wines, luxury automobiles, pearls and furs. Nothing is too dear, henceforth, for humans! Everyone covets the broad life, facile amour, rare pleasures, exotic visions and the sensualized fatigue of dancing, and the dreamy annihilation of drunkenness, and the surprising fever of traveling.

One wants to relive a thousand lives by reading the lives of great men, great criminals, and great adventurers, reviving great amours, great revolutions, and great disasters.

One shakes the past in order to extract pleasure from it, one exhausts the present, one anticipates the future. The invisible orchestras that electricity causes to unfurl in mysterious sheets over the entire surface of the planet beats time to the infinity of the immense sabbat that Europe is leading, extenuating pleasure during the night—drinking, making love, banqueting in the exorbitant delirium of speed, avidity and risk.

Where does it come from, then, this reckless acceleration of human existence, this madness of the senses, this leap beyond the limits that mark a new era?

Has the war, by chance, poured out for us a seed of cantharides, inoculated a microbe of St. Vitus' dance, imposed an obsession with immediate enjoyment, a madness of acquisition, spending, emotion, of monstrous sensation? Have men emerged from the trenches more lustful, more insatiable and more materialistic?

Or else...

Is it not also true that all these people who are dancing and embracing, eating and rolling around, whining and coveting, have a strange gaze at times? Would one not say that human eyes have never been as sickeningly expressive as during certain pauses in the dance that Europe is currently leading?

Sometimes, returning from the Bourse or from a voyage, in the arms of his mistress or supping in a tavern, does not the face of many a pleasure-seeker suddenly collapse, as if a death-mask has fallen into dust and another, more ancient, returns from I know not what Hell to burst forth for the space of a second?

On gazing at close range, on observing with care the modern man, one suspects a horrible secret that he is trying to hide. As long as he is living close to light, pearls, smiles, the sound of banjos, under the influence of wine, in the proximity of women, that still goes on. But when, by mistake, he finds himself confronted by Nature, plains and dawns, or even by a mirror, one might think that he is risking, in spite of his determination, remembering and examining himself.

For, in sum, why that sudden distress, those dilated pupils, the anguish of those clenched teeth, the rigidity of those parted lips?

What do they see, by what are they suddenly visited, those speculators, those dancers, those arrivistes, those bluffers?

Don't ask them. They will look at you like somnambulists awakening to another life, and they will return, laughing and smiling, to flirtation, to calculation, to movement, to pleasure.

They will return to forgetfulness.

But, for the space of a second, you will have glimpsed on their face a haggard expression, more singular than dolorous, an expression of fear produced by an immense emptiness, a plunge into the abyss, an annihilation of the soul. It an expression almost similar to the one you might have imagined on the features of the Spanish Lover on perceiving the dead return to demand account of his debauchery, or on the face of the man who, in order to have a little more youth, has given up his soul, or the other who, which the blow of an ax, spilled fraternal blood, the *first blood*...

Martigny interrupted his reading and closed the notebook. He retained it in his hands for a few moments, hesitantly. Then, without reopening it, he approached the fireplace slowly and cast it into the flames.

IV

The next day, Martigny went to see his daughter, who lived in a silent and dilapidated town house on the Quasi d'Orléans.

He knew the state worse than mourning in which he would find Antoinette, fallen back into solitude and anxiety after the brief escape into wellbeing that the consciousness of the imminent future had tinted with tragedy.

The young woman was, in fact, hiding her face in her hands, and tears were trickling slowly but incessantly along her fingers when her father came into her room.

"What obscurity!" he exclaimed. "Are you here, Antoinette?"

Receiving a sob as his only response, he went to open the windows and contemplated the tearful woman under the sudden influx of light. He ran to her.

"I saw Maurice yesterday evening, and I put him on his train," he said, upset by that other dolor but speaking first in order not to submit to questions about his heartrending conversation with the soldier.

"When will he be able to come back?" groaned the young woman in a voice pierced by something infantile. "He's going to be in the front line again. They might be attacked at any day."

Martigny gazed at her with a tender sadness, avoiding a response.

She continued: "If you knew how good it has been, Papa! I understood. On seeing him again, that I couldn't continue to exist if he were no longer there. But I found him so changed that it frightened me. He was very tender, even more tender than usual, if that's possible. Sometimes, a haggard expression passed through his eyes, as if they had been suddenly struck by I know not what horrible vision."

Antoinette burst into sobs again. Then, she raised her head and considered Martigny with despair, who remained silent, his fists clenched.

"Answer me, Father! Tell me, you who know more than others about everything, what I have to do in order not to lose him."

"What do you want me to say, my child? We're playthings in the hands of Destiny. We have no control over life and death. There's nothing but hope—that's all."

"But then, if humans turn away in that fashion, declaring their impotence, those who are suffering must address themselves elsewhere."

"Yes, my child," Martigny replied. "Let them address themselves elsewhere, if they believe that they can find consolation there."

"In that case, I want to learn to pray, Papa. I shall implore the one who never abandons. Nowadays, the church has become the refuge of the afflicted. There, the great hope is nestled. And more than the churches, it is souls that are being transformed into as many sanctuaries. In France, in Europe, everywhere people are suffering—which is to say, the entire world—people are reaching out toward heaven.

She had grasped her father's knees recklessly.

"Pray, my dear," Martigny replied. "I would pray too, if I could. And after having prayed, come and rest your head on my bosom. Above all, don't forget that you're all I have in the world. You're my mainstay, and my life depends on yours."

"Tomorrow afternoon," the young woman went on, pursuing her idea, "I intend to take part in the feminine procession, the procession of wives, widows and mothers, which is going to hold vigil all night on the Plaine Saint-Denis to implore celestial aid. And it won't only be in Paris that people are praying that night. In every city in France, England, Italy and the Balkans, and also, undoubtedly, among the enemy—in Russia, Germany and America—mutilated souls and disabled beings, all the women who are waiting in dread, will lift up their hearts and their arms, to request from God what humans can no longer give.

"It's evident," said Martigny, "That if there is anything that can move Heaven, it will be that prayer, the cry of distress that will rise from the entire surface of the world toward the Eternal. In the same way that no scourge has ever equaled the one that is striking the earth today, never has such a unanimous appeal been addressed by the Creator's creatures. So I believe that the imploration of hearts ravaged by tears, souls blackened by mourning, might be capable of stirring divine mercy. For that, only one thing is necessary..."

"What?"

"For God to exist, my child."

PART TWO: AND THE MIRACLE HAP-PENED

I

The miracle of the cessation of the war was accomplished on 25 December 1949, at the approach of night.

That evening, Martigny was attending a party that Madame Perrin, the president of the godmothers of the war, was giving in honor of the wife of General Jourdinot.

Tea was being served and slices of black bread, although white bread was still available for a few more days. Madame Perrin thought that the color was in accord with that of souls.

She was complaisant about that.

"It's necessary not to eat white bread while they're fighting out there," she said. To which she added: "It's the least of equalities to be content with black bread, participating by that privation in the afflictions of the fatherland. I hope, too, that it's in the same respectable sentiment that the government will suppress patisseries."

Madame Larrivan shared that opinion. "I desire, she said, her eyes wide, "that we lack everything."

"But it's an unnecessary sacrifice," said Mademoiselle Caumardon, who, separated from her fiancé, was distressed by the prolongation of the war.

"All sacrifices are unnecessary," replied Madame Perrin, severely.

Martigny leaned toward his friend's ear and murmured to him: "Did you hear that? Madame Perrin, who ordinarily talks in order to say nothing, has just pronounced a verity. She has done so, moreover, without perceiving it, and it's necessary not to hold it against her. How true that is, and how remarkable it is! Sacrifices are profitable neither to the gods nor humans. That's why we accomplish them when we're terrified and believe that we can't obtain what we desire by any sane means."

Meanwhile, Madame Cornut had come into the room and, while the floorboards creaked under her insupportable weight, her voice was already yapping: "Can anyone tell me where Sannard is? Since this morning, the idea has been trotting through my head that he must be under cover somewhere. At any rate, he's keeping his head down, and the bearded and bespectacled fellow has never inspired confidence or sympathy in me."

"I believe that he is, in fact, safely ensconced in a hospital in Marseille," Madame Larrivan tried to assure her.

But Mademoiselle Caumardon explained that no one had heard any further mention of Monsieur Sannard simply because he had fallen on the field of honor in the course of a reconnaissance mission near Luneville in September."

"The one of who is well and truly under cover is our friend Mazelle," said Madame Larrivan, in order to recover lost ground. "Discharged under the pretext of internal varicose veins, he hasn't budged from the département of the Haute-Savoie. I met him on the summit of Mont Blanc. With his hirsute beard and his bulging eyes, while the clouds flowed by beneath his feet, he seemed to be proceeding to the Last Judgment

"I'm going to inscribe him in my notebook," said Madame Perrin softly. And she took a pencil out of her handbag.

"You're keeping a list of those under cover, Madame?" Martigny asked her, admiringly.

"Only friends," Madame Perrin specified. "The others don't interest me. But for friends, it might be useful, after the war. Anyway, I'll read it to you, my list. It's not secret, and you might find people you know on it."

Martigny declined the offer. "Child, I've never been able to remember the names of the Kings of France," he said, by way of excuse. "I always stopped at Dagobert. Now that my memory's getting weaker by the day, how do you expect me to remember the list of those under cover?"

Madame Perrin said that she wanted the cowards to be branded with a hot iron, in order that they might be distinguished. Then, regretfully changing the subject, she asked Martigny if he had heard Père Duplex, who was preaching at the Madeleine.

"He's so full of enthusiasm, so bellicose," she added, "that they're calling him Abbé la Victoire."

Martigny confessed that he did not go to church.

"I envy you for still having the courage to go to mass, Madame," he told her. "It's evident that you have a candid soul full of piety. For myself, in spite of my taste for pomp and ceremony, I've resolved not to enter a church again so long as we're occupied in feeding on human flesh and slandering our brethren. Strictly speaking, one could insult Jehovah without shame, in view of the fact that the odor of blood has always been agreeable to his nostrils; but for gentle Jesus—the true God of Christians—it seems to me that I'd be very embarrassed to extend red hands toward him and address words to him."

Instead of replying, Madame Perrin precipitated toward the door of the drawing room in order to welcome the wife of General Jourdinot, the principal attraction of the gathering, whom everyone wanted to see.

Scarcely received before the war, forgotten in corners and papering the walls, the general's wife had become interesting and precious since the opening of hostilities. Her husband was in command of the army in Poland. And in the same fashion as certain gold stocks poorly quoted on the Bourse, which rise vertiginously when a seam is discovered in the mine, the general's wife had acquired great prestige between one day and the next. The president of five societies, discreetly applauded when she came into gatherings, she was, moreover, a kind of oracle of events.

The guests hastened around her with deference and curiosity, and asked for her news. Prudently, however, stiffened under the weight of the responsibilities that weighed upon her husband, and knowing, on the other hand, that mystery heightens prestige, she showed herself to be optimistic, vague and aleatory.

Baronne Lehmann, on the contrary, who entered in her turn and who, thanks to Sir John MacPerson, was assumed to know the English plans, seemed slightly more communicative.

"If, at the moment, the English are retreating again, it's in order better to conform to the plan," she declared. "It's only a strategic retreat."

"Doubtless they want to draw the enemy as much as possible toward the center," Madame Larrivan objected, injudiciously.

"The victory is only a matter of a few more months," said the Baronne, imperturbably.

"Is it really MacPerson who wrote that to you?" Martigny could not prevent himself from asking.

"No," the Baronne admitted, frankly. "You understand the reserve that MacPerson must maintain. But I saw Annie Péchin yesterday, who is, I dare say, the foremost seer in the world. She has so much fluid that one receives a shock merely by touching her hand. Now, she's held a séance at the home of a highly placed financier. Having fallen into a trance, Annie was transported to the front, into the middle of the battle. She described the assault on Warsaw to us precisely, of which we read the report in the following day's communiqué. Can you imagine that she saw, clearly, Spirits floating above the combatants? The Spirits of the allies were all white, while those moving over the Russians were as black as coal."

"And with regard to the end of the war, what did Annie Péchin predict?"

"It will end in May, without fail," the Baronne replied. "The dictator von Herskin will go mad, and the English will enter Berlin while we march on Moscow."

That prediction was welcomed by a favorable murmur.

"But why the English in Berlin and not us?" interrogated the intransigent Madame Larrivan, not without some reproach.

"I can only repeat to you what the somnambulist predicted," the Baronne replied, with a gesture that expressed regret at not being able to do more. Then she added: "It's confidentially that I'm communicating this news here. I know that nothing will leak outside."

"You're right, Madame," said Martigny. "One can't be too suspicious. How many enemy ears are listening to us when we talk among friends!"

But General Jourdinot's wife opined in her turn that it was necessary not to joke and that there were many more spies in the country than one might believe.

"Only yesterday I encountered two in the Metro," said Madame Larrivan. "I didn't hesitate to run to warn the commissariat, but God only knows whether they'll find them..."

People approved, and someone asked her how she had recognized them.

"Merely by looking at their faces, one was edified," Madame Larrivan explained. "Shifty eyes, hair s blonde as wheat, and spectacles. I'll add that they were speaking an unknown language, very harsh on the ear, which could only be Russian. But what confirmed my suspicions is that they were in such haste to get off at the next station."

Then everyone began talking about suspect Slavs they had encountered since the commencement of the war. They had been seen everywhere: on trains, on the roads, at crossroads and in the forests. People were convinced that the spas were overflowing with them, as well as the beaches

At the moment when everyone was rushing toward the buffet, Martigny was joined by Léry, who appeared very perplexed.

Since the beginning of the war, the paleographer had had a bewildered expression. He seemed to be incessantly waking up from a somnambulistic sleep and collected sinister news like aeroliths that had taken him by surprise while deciphering a palimpsest.

"Can you explain to me," he asked Martigny, why one no longer encounters Mademoiselle Fleuriot here, the daughter of our great Fleuriot, who discovered the antituberculosis serum? I've just asked Madame Perrin what has become of her, and do you know what she replied to me, in her glacial tone: 'It's not in my house that *that person* will ever be seen again.'"

"Madame Perrin was right," said Martigny. "The question you were asking was improper, not to say immoral. You're the only person who doesn't know that Mademoiselle Fleuriot has recently acquired a very bad reputation. Can you imagine that she as caught kissing a soldier on the lips in the English hospital in the Rue d'Ulm."

"You're joking, Martigny," Léry exclaimed. "Mademoiselle Fleuriot, who is thirty-five years old and the daughter of an illustrious man, has spent the greater part of her fortune since the beginning of the war on benevolent works. She has served as a nurse in Champagne and the Vosges, always choosing the most dangerous and the most difficult posts. I know few soldiers who deserve the medal of honor as much as she does."

"She does good with simplicity and by natural inclination—but that lack of effort already seems rather singular and inspires envy. Then again, being spontaneous, Mademoiselle Fleuriot has gone so far as to kiss the young wounded soldier for whom she was caring in the hospital in the Rue d'Ulm. Unfortunately, she was seen and her action was interpreted malevolently. It's necessary not to forget that the lady patronesses are no longer young and they like to avenge themselves as they can for their husbands' infidelities. In any case, the fact was related to the directress, and Mademoiselle Fleuriot has been struck off the list of nurses."

"What a pity!" exclaimed Léry.

"You're wrong," said Martigny, in a tone of reprimand. "We're more severe than ever on the morality of sexual relations. We do well. Don't forget, my dear friend, that sexual morality is the only morality that remains to us. In times of peace there is interindividual morality, but in times of war, the only one of the ten commandments that remains standing is the fifth—the one that forbids disorderly relations between the sexes. You know how society has transformed that one: *Thou shalt not allow thyself to be caught while thou art with thy neighbor's wife.* On that chapter, we're intractable. Madame Perrin, for example, watches pitilessly over the relations of the sexes. 'It's the least sacrifice we can make for those at the front, to deprive ourselves of the pleasures of amour,' she declared once again the other day. To which Mademoiselle Caumardon, who suspects her fiancé of forgetting her out there, replied: 'Let Messieurs the soldiers be the first to do so!'"

"Then you condemn Mademoiselle Fleuriot for having given her fortune, her time and her late nights?" asked Léry.

Martigny considered his friend for a long time with his moist and black gaze.

"Is it in my habits to condemn? I leave that iniquitous métier to the judges. I dare not even pardon or absolve. For, have you remarked, Léry, that in pardoning, we suppose ourselves superior to those whom we heap with our indulgence? Now, we are all equally fallible, ignorant, blind, and submissive to the hazards of Destiny, miserable victims of passion. We all advance like a herd led by egotism, we all meditate doing, and we do, what we would like to forbid to others. No, I don't criticize Mademoiselle Fleuriot. I will even kiss her hand respectfully at the next opportunity, firstly because her hand is beautiful, and secondly because in granting a kiss without amour to a young soldier, she was making a sublime gift in conformity with the admirable examples of Christian legend, equaling Saint Madeleine, Saint Thaïs and, above all, Saint Mary the Egyptian—the one who first proved to us that in abandoning one's body without desire, one is accomplishing a passion like Jesus, a sacrifice of immolation."

As Martigny pronounced those words, a violent subterranean shock shook the drawing room. The old man was projected into the arms of his interlocutor.

A kind of panic ensued.

"A bomb!" was cried on all sides.

But as the shock continued, Madame Caumardon said, daring to open the window: "It's more likely an earthquake." She immediately uttered a cry of astonishment mingled with admiration. "Look! Look!" she exclaimed.

Everyone ran on to the balcony.

At first, they did not speak, so gripping was the spectacle, surpassing human anticipations.

A kind of living and brilliant aurora was illuminating the sky, which seemed transformed into an immense diaphanous pearl, mysteriously inflamed. Against that precious background, rainbows were deployed in profusion, dissolving and degrading all colors and adding a miraculous opulence, as if ablaze with opal of a candid and pure nacreous splendor.

"What's that?" said Martigny, searching his intellectual, logical and scientific universe in vain for an explanation of the phenomenon. Then, turning to Jean Astarot, who was an astronomer, he asked him: "Could that be the light of a meteor?"

"It's not local, it's not sidereal, it has neither a center nor limits," the scientist replied. "From the astronomical viewpoint, it's incomprehensible.

"Might it be the projection of a monstrous luminous fire?"

"A projection has a center of emanation," Astarot replied. "No, this surpasses my knowledge. It must be the end of the world."

A rumor was rising from everywhere. Windows opened and people who had descended into the street communicated their admiration and dread to one another.

By degrees, the light diminished, the great reflections were extinguished, and only the light of a permanent aurora subsisted on the horizon.

When Madame Perrin's guests went back inside from the balcony and looked at one another in the lamplight, a new exclamation sprang from all mouths. One might have thought that an imprint of the celestial radiation remained imprinted on their faces.

"Look at Madame Perrin!" said Martigny, alarmed, to his friend Léry. "One wouldn't recognize her, so benevolent is her expression…"

"And Madame Larrivan," replied Léry. "Her lips have lost their thinness, her face is no longer haggard and she seems majestic in the strength of mildness. Previously, I found resemblances with a portrait of Torquemada I once saw, but it's now Francis of Assisi of whom she reminds me."

After a pause, he added: "Besides which, I'm also experiencing a great change within myself. One might think that a new man is taking possession of my envelope. Other ideas, and another consciousness, are taking possession of me." On which, leaning toward Martigny's ear, he said: "I confess that for the first time in my life, I'm afraid. For I don't understand..."

"Yes, indeed; we're entering into the unintelligible," murmured Martigny. "I too feel transformed."

And as Léry begged him to look in order to tell him whether his face bore traces of the change, he replied, smiling: "Not as much as the mistress of the house. You weren't malevolent, my poor Léry, and it didn't require a veritable metamorphosis for you to represent good will—but you're radiant now, that's all."

With that, without taking part in the passionate commentaries that were being exchanged in the drawing-room, he left in order to go home.

On the way he thought: *Léry was afraid. And for the first time in my life, I feel that, strictly speaking, it would be possible for me to pray...*

II

The next day, the newspapers were full of accounts of the prodigy, and also signaled its immense repercussions.

What had happened on the battlefield was beyond any anticipation.

However, the day had commenced like any other day.

In spite of the litanies that had been sung the day before in the two hemispheres, the struggle had resumed more ardently and more furiously. The cruel von Ebinck had given the order for a general attack. Cannons as big as cathedrals bellowed incessantly, airships projected death, and a host of German soldiers littered the edges of the occidental trenches. The troops were marching in bloody mud, slipping on human brain-tissue.

And it was at the end of that attack that the miracle occurred.

The soldiers recounted that in the middle of the palpitating night, a shock had suddenly shaken the trenches and a blinding light comparable to a boreal aurora had ripped through the obscurity. Suddenly, everything was supernaturally colored. The trees in the valley appeared coral and saffron, the sky was limpid and sapphire, and the birds started to sing recklessly, as they do on mild spring mornings.

At the same time, the Germans who were advancing dropped their weapons and the artillerists felt incapable of directing their weapons, while, for their part, the Latins emerged from the retrenchments as if dread and prudence had vanished from their minds like a dream.

The leaders, German as well as French, who were occupied in giving orders, having lost the memory of the hatred that had dictated them, stood as if paralyzed.

And the immense armies, irreconcilable a few seconds before, marched to meet one another. Those who had previously been attacking, advancing to destroy and disembowel, now seemed to be following a peaceful procession, olive-branch in hand. In different languages but understanding one another by heart, Caucasians and Kalmucks, Iberians and Celts, Saxons and Latins, those with snub noses and those with blond hair and blue eyes, affirmed their fraternity and gave one another the kiss of peace.

The instincts of the ferocious beast were now succeeded in the human mind by the mildness of the gazelle and the innocent purity of the turtle-dove.

That was accomplished in a few seconds, the sudden change in consciousness taking place simultaneously all over the immense field of carnage. In the depths of the Alps, in the Argonne and even on the coasts of Japan and the two Americas, in Russia as in Belgium, an equal mildness, a similar tenderness disarmed human beings.

The meteorological phenomenon that announced the miracle had appeared at midnight. Five minutes later, the destructive engines were lying idle, deprived of the animating will that had previously communicated human malevolence to them.

And the same ineffable disturbance of souls that had pacified the battlefields also operated in the cities among the citizens.

The newspapers of the entire world affirmed that, in the hearts of sovereigns, in the brains of military leaders and governments as well as individuals, all hatred had been extinguished. The wellsprings of good will, for-

giveness and amour gushed forth everywhere and unanimously.

III

At eleven o'clock in the morning. Martigny was still in the process of reading the astonishing news when Jacques Sarravin, a journalist on the staff of *Le Temps*, was announced, who, once introduced, asked for an interview.

"We would like, my dear master, to have your opinion one the recent events to which the public have been subjected, without daring either to judge them or grasp their meaning. We journalists are inventive, but I confess to you that I have renounced writing a single line of worthwhile explanation on what happened yesterday evening."

"Have you interrogated the men of science?" asked Martigny.

"The scientists declare that they are unable to understand any of it, and the politicians, naturally, are no further advanced."

"But then, if the events are incomprehensible to everyone," Martigny replied, "it's necessary to think that norms have changed and that the earth is steering toward a new orient."

"What do you mean?"

"I mean that, according to all evidence, a philter, an unknown leaven, is in the process of operating on the mentality of the planet. It's undeniable that someone is raising meteoric phenomena, changing the course of the stars and disarming hands."

"Nothing is truer," Sarravin replied, promptly. "But who can that someone be? That's the question."

And the reporter looked at Martigny impatiently, through the lenses of his spectacles. His effeminate, clean-shaven face, permanently colored by the usage of hard liquor, expressed the most anxious curiosity.

"Since the scientists," the dramatist continued, "can't explain the event in accordance with the physical order and the logicians remain stupefied, it's necessary to conclude that it surpasses the laws of matter and the horizons of human intellect."

"But in that case…?"

"In that case, my dear Monsieur, it's simply a matter of a miracle, of a supraterrestrial intervention, the intermission of a particular will that is manifest in overturning the natural order wholesale."

"And who would be capable of that miracle?" Sarravin persisted.

"Someone, probably, whose powers are unlimited and who can play with consciences as well as constellations, someone who manipulates the impossible and is careless of laws, the laws being submissive to him."

Sarravin listened, mute; so Martigny went on: "What other, I ask you, would be capable of insufflating, in the space of a lightning-flash, peace into the hearts of men and transforming wolves into lambs? Until now, he has not given the slightest sign of existence, but it is appropriate to believe that, after having abandoned the Earth created by his hands to the mercy of Fatality, he has finally deigned to listen to its suffering."

Then, without allowing Sarravin, whose eyes were shining recklessly, to reply, he added: "I deduce therefrom that you can announce to your readers as very probable that God is realized, that God is manifest. As in the story of Genesis, he has just mingled with humans and answered their prayers. Henceforth, the world will no longer be living its history, but its apocalypse."

Jacques Sarravin, who had started taking notes feverishly, hesitated momentarily, and then objected:

"I'm transcribing faithfully, my dear master, and will immediately send an account of this interview to the printer. Your opinion is authoritative. However, I won't publish your words without a certain dread. Although conservative, *Le Temps* is a republican newspaper, disengaged from all superstition. We are liberal and conciliatory toward the Church, of course, but we don't want to pass for clerics. The boss who sent me will be stupefied when he learns that you, a freethinker, not to say an atheist..."

Martigny interrupted him, getting to his feet. "Pardon me, Monsieur. I was an atheist as long as God did not show himself. No one had ever seen him or sensed him until yesterday. But when he has done what he has done now, even *Le Temps* can change its attitude without compromise. Be tranquil. No one will accuse you of corruption. While transmuting hearts and overturning the planets, the Eternal has only employed licit means thus far."

With that, saluting Jacques Sarravin, Martigny went to see Antoinette, who, drunk with joy, cried to him:

"He's come back, Papa...Maurice has come back! And if you could see his beautiful serene face... decidedly, happy days are about to recommence."

IV

Soon, everyone shared Martigny's opinion.

Nevertheless, it is necessary to admit that the divine manifestation troubled, and deflected, but did not transform, human habits.

The early days that followed the miracle were full of stupefaction. Newspapers were snatched from vendors' hands in the hope of finding news therein. For the first time, however, the audacity of the reporters and the varied resources of the great dailies could not satisfy, or even deceive, the curiosity of the readers.

In vain, the wireless telegraph systems launched waves and caused their sparks to crackle.

No divine mediation, not the slightest celestial novelty, came to astonish the world.

"I'd pay two hundred, three hundred thousand francs for a single word from Him," said the editor of the *Aurore* to his faithful Prude.

To which Prude, who had succeeded in interviewing the Emperor of the new Chinese dynasty in his porcelain palace, and Coco, the murderer of twenty-four little girls, on the scaffold, Prude, who had been able to discover, three hours before the agents of the Sûreté, the trail of Père Lafourchette and obtain the memoirs of the ex-Queen of England, started caressing his beard in a gesture of humiliated perplexity.

"If I only knew where he could be found," he murmured, angrily. "I'd go to the Devil to pinch him..."

"Start by visiting Rome, Constantinople, Mecca and Benares," the editor replied. "See the Pope, the Patriarch, the Mufti. Perhaps someone can inform you..."

And while the reporters were agitating, the people waited.

Everyone was impatient to elucidate exactly to what extent the new state of affairs might be profitable to him. The churches were overflowing with people, the number of curés was insufficient to meet the demand for masses and prayers. From all parts, prayers sprang in floods toward the heavens. Everyone demanded a particular miracle from the Almighty. Everyone wanted God to sort out his personal affairs, favor his amours, or enable him to gain money.

Every morning, on getting up, people hoped for a new manifestation, a new prodigy. And as, since Christmas, nothing supernatural had occurred, the impatient world, enticed by the miraculous, remained suspended between expectation and disappointment.

V

"It's necessary to recognize," Martigny said to his friend Astarot one afternoon, "that the government and the clergy seem rather disappointed by this enormous terrestrial event."

"It's incontestable, in any case," the astronomer replied, "that the politicians and the leaders of the religious authorities, previously in dissent in the Latin countries, are getting closer to one another."

"That's because politicians and priests see themselves equally wronged and threatened by the sudden intrusion of God in their affairs," replied Martigny. "A God who makes peace and disarms nations without consulting either dictators, the presidents of republics or diplomats; a God who liberates himself from the mediation of any church and appears to people directly, without being channeled through a sanctuary; a God, finally, who shakes all religious prestige, is an inconvenient God, a creator of difficulties, a disturber of the order of things."

"What provokes great polemics in particular is the identity of the acting God," said Astarot, wiping the lenses of his spectacles. "Is it old Yahweh?"

"There you're raising a much debated problem, although insensate, in my opinion," said Martigny, "for I am, in fact, naïve enough to believe that the God in question was quite simply God."

"When you say God, however, you're not saying anything. It's necessary to choose. The Protestants affirm that it must be the one of the Bible, the Catholics the Christ, the Hindus—who are so well led and whom

172

England wants to keep—sustain with loud cries that it can be only be a question of the manifestation of Buddha, while, for their part, the Muslims opt for Allah."

"I don't understand how, in debating what one does not know, that one can become irritated to such a degree—because it's necessary to recognize that the excitation of minds is extreme."

"It comes from the fact that everyone is amorous of his own opinion and intends to hold as real what he desires. We saw enough of the reign of that mentality during the war."

"Between the three Christian churches—the Catholic, the Protestant and the Orthodox—the arguments are even more bitter and envenomed," said Martigny. "Those three cults scarcely differ and, being in accord on the essentials, are by virtue of that very fact irreconcilable. Each of the three churches would rather admit the triumph of Beelzebub than that of one of the opposing churches."

At that moment Antoinette came in, holding a copy of the *Aurore* in her hand.

"Papa, here's the report of a sensational interview with Monsignor Novatelli, the papal nuncio. Prude has succeeded in making His Holiness submit to an interrogation, through the intermediary of the nuncio."

"And what does he say?" asked Martigny, indifferently.

"His Holiness counsels the faithful to hold themselves in readiness. Until further notice, he has declared, an event that emerged from outside the rules and disrupts all habits must remain outside the Church. That's why the Pope has refused to convene a council. Furthermore, after the interview, Monsignor Novatelli went much further. Would you like me to read you the end of Prude's article?

"I'm not opposed to it," said Martigny.

Antoinette read:

"'The God of our father had been adored and has shined until now by inaction,' His Eminence confided to me. 'Why imagine that he would suddenly change?'

"I ventured to object to him the apparition on Sinai, the sun stopped by Joshua and Balaam's ass.

"'All those miracles, Monsignor Novatelli replied, 'were accomplished a very long time ago, and always by the intermediary of priests, prophets or saints. It was Moses, Joshua or Balaam who operated in the cases you cite. That is precisely why we reproach present events, which have been produced without our having any warning. For it is necessary to distinguish between miracles, Monsieur, and be wary. The Devil also made some, in the Middle Ages...'

"'Do you believe,' I asked His Eminence, 'that it is the Devil who put a stop to the war?'

"Monseigneur Novatelli retained a reserved attitude with regard to that question, which is easily explicable. 'I'm not accusing anyone,' he hastened to declare, as he rose to his feet, 'but let us say clearly that, until further orders, the Vatican regards the miracle as not having happened.'"

After Antoinette had ceased reading, Astarot spoke.

"Evidently, the Pope is very perplexed. I can understand it, however. Put yourself in his place. How can one dare to declare that one is infallible when anything might happen tomorrow to give him the lie?"

VI

One day, Léry came into Martigny's study like a gust of wind.

"Well, what do you think of the great news?"

"What news?"

"God has finally deigned to manifest himself to humans via the intermediary of Marie Fleuriot. You know her, since it was you who told me that she was thrown out of the hospital in the Rue d'Ulm for having given a kiss to a wounded soldier."

Martigny replied that he knew Marie Fleuriot very well, that she had an angelic face, but that he doubted that she was the spokesperson for the divine will.

"Every day," he added, there are two or three sensational announcements in *Le Petit Parisien* and *La Croix* by prophetesses or illuminates who affirm that they have been visited by God. In these times of delirium, it's wise to be on one's guard."

"I'm no more credulous than you, Martigny. In spite of the absence of malice and hypocrisy that characterizes Marie Fleuriot and inspires respect in me, I remained very skeptical with regard to her mission. Nevertheless, it's necessary to yield to the evidence. Marie has worked miracles. Prude, who was shouting at her door and tried to extort an interview from her by force lost the use of speech for twenty-four hours, which was a cruel privation for him. Others experienced violent shocks on touching her and have seen flames around her."

"Is that all?" said Martigny, impassively.

"No, that isn't all. Yesterday, an extraordinary event occurred, a public miracle, in a full session of the Senate. It can't be attributed to suggestion. They had heard Balmy, the former minister who, having made a visit to Marie Fleuriot, invited the government to take into consideration the proposals of the inspired young woman—proposals already accepted by England and Germany. Then Fargot, the President of the Council, who doesn't forget his electors of the quarter of Vieilles Audriettes, who have confided him with a radical-socialist mandate, got up to reject the proposals, attack what he called "superstitious guidance" and propose a motion of confidence. And at the very moment when he began to speak, he felt an abrupt commotion that threw him to the ground. The glass of water that was on the lectern tipped over him. The President nevertheless got up and tried to recommence his speech—but again he was knocked over supernaturally. So, the third time, he didn't persist, and Marie Fleuriot's proposals were accepted by a show of hands."

"What are these proposals?"

"God announces, through the mouth of the inspired woman, that he has a message to transmit to the peoples of the earth. He will communicate it to them before a universal assembly in which the leading intellectuals and the natural leaders of the various nations must take part."

"I suppose it's been decided, then?"

"Given that freethinking France no longer opposes any difficulties, it only remained to choose the place of the gathering and the date. Furthermore, it has been announced his morning that, in order to cut short rivalries, Marie has declared that, on the basis of divine inspiration, she has designated Paris as the seat of the assembly, and the amphitheater of the old Sorbonne. People from all countries will come in pilgrimage to take part in it."

"We'll see…," said Martigny, plunged in his meditations. "I can distinguish less and less clearly where we're going. But in any case, it's new and unexpected. The history of the planet, which has been dull until now, has the appearance of turning into a feuilleton."

VII

From then on, faith in Marie Fleuriot was consolidated and amplified.

Everyone had abandoned skepticism, all the more so as the young woman had declared, at the opening of the congress, that God would affirm himself by new miracles.

People therefore waited anxiously.

Marie had conquered the popularity of a Jeanne d'Arc, or a Catherine of Siena. Her door was besieged, favors and cures were demanded of her.

Some solicitors came to beg her to reveal the number that would allow them to win at roulette, others to beg her to restore the fidelity of their mistress. Her friends boasted about knowing her, citing her by her forename, and there was no talk in drawing rooms of anyone but her.

In brief, Marie became more celebrated than the generals and the ministers, overshadowing with her popularity the dancers from Borneo who were all the rage at the moment, the flautists of the Canary Islands, and even the handsome Monsieur Fanfalot who, during the war, had made a billion dealing in coal and had spent half of it on luminous advertisements glorifying him and his business.

As Marie's door was not open to anyone, however, as she did not receive any of her friends and had refused the presidency of the Prix Femina, which had been offered to her, people ended up criticizing her and deploring the Lord's choice.

"I have the impression," Martigny concluded at Madame Perrin's one day, "that people are accusing God of a certain lack of tact."

"That's what people are saying, and I find it just," replied the mistress of the house. "It's because the divine election is incomprehensible. For after all, there are many celebrated men and many great orators who could have exercised that supreme sacerdocy brilliantly. And then, there was the Pope..."

"You're forgetting, my dear friend," Martigny objected, "that we don't know whether God is Christian."

"Even supposing," Madame Perrin continued, imperturbably, "that God wanted at any price to make use of a woman, why didn't he choose the Princesse de Clairval, our great poet, or the Baronne de Brunde, who presides over so many works of charity and receives the five Academies in her home, or even Madame Fanfar, a former Miss Europe, whose marvelous beauty is matched with irreproachable conduct. Those are personalities who would certainly have served, and even heightened, divine prestige..."

"But what tells you, my dear Madame, that God wants to heighten his prestige? For myself, I suspect that he doesn't care about it. He ought to want to heighten his prestige as little as to lower it. You're placing God on a level with Monsieur Dusol, the President of the Republic, or Noel Lloyd, who governs our neighbors with so much success. That's already an elevated rank—but I fear that it might not be high enough."

"You'll grant me, however, Monsieur Martigny, that a demoiselle who was talked about before the war...God must insist on chastity..."

"Does one ever know? If he's so insistent on it, he hasn't given us the desire for it. As for our other objec-

179

tions, they don't seem to me to be any more valid. You reproach Marie Fleuriot for being humble. Perhaps it's sufficient for God that she has a good heart..."

Léry, who was present, supported his friend. "Yes, in sum," he murmured, why shouldn't the good and the poor be among the Elect?"

"I wonder that myself," exclaimed Martigny, smiling. "All the more so because, in all times, it's to them that he has promised Heaven in order to console them for being deprived of all material wealth. But to tell the truth, we accord them eternal life in order to be able to keep terrestrial enjoyments, which appear to us to be far more certain, for our own usage, without scruple."

PART THREE: THE SPIRIT OF GOD VISITS THE EARTH

I

On 14 January 1950, on a miraculously and expressly spring-like day, the ecumenical assembly was held at which God, for the first time, communicated with his creatures.

The great amphitheater of the Sorbonne was overflowing with guests. In the vestibule, the Rue des Ecoles and the adjacent streets all the way to the Quai Saint-Michel, people gathered, dazed by expectation and incomprehension.

A few newspapers had demanded that the assembly be held at the Champ de Mars, in order that the public could take part in the prodigious session, to which Marie Fleuriot had responded impolitely that God was not speaking for all but exclusively for the comprehending. Otherwise, the young woman said, being the creator of everything, he would also have summoned the horses, cats and weasels.

There was then thought of introducing to the assembly diplomats, ministers and députés. The inspired one opposed it, objecting that fine and clever talkers could not be of any utility there. She only admitted kings and heads of state, not because she held them in particular consideration, she explained, but because of their authority, which would permit them to transmit the divine will to the crowds.

Then, Marie chose certain individuals from the two worlds that she did not know, but whom her inspiration suggested as appropriate to form the total mirror in which human aspirations would be reflected.

Once the members were designated, she was much more accommodating with regard to the audience, and even left the care of sending out the invitations to the rector of the university. So one quickly saw displayed in the amphitheater a mixture of beauty and hideousness, sparkling pretty faces accompanied by rich bankers and young actors enchained to rich sexagenarians whose wrinkled necks were streaming with pals: all the ill-assorted couples that compose European high society. And the assembly where God was to manifest himself definitely bore more resemblance to an Opera gala than Mount Tabor.

Marie was the last to enter. Petite in stature, her eyes emitting soft flames, her gestures hieratical, she was comparable to those almost floral beings that Fra Angelico left, by way of a testament, on the walls of the Florentine convent of San Marco. A murmur of surprise welcomed her, and the women were poorly impressed by the simplicity of her gray dress, devoid of a belt.

The representatives of the various nations had charged Noel Lloyd, the president of England, the American novelist Sir Oliver Test and the French philosopher Jules Vibret, the celebrated theoretician of immutable destiny, to harangue the inspired one.

Marie responded with a few infinitely humble words, which, pronounced in her musical voice, soothed the auditorium and evoked dear voices, fresh voices of children returning from the past.

Then, turning toward the leader of the English Republic, she said:

"Monsieur Noel Lloyd, I designate you as the president of this assembly, because I divine that you desire it.

And after the president had taken his place, radiant and saying that he was only accepting the responsibility because the honor would rebound on his country, Marie began to speak.

She announced that God, in spite of his seasons, had spread that day the perfume of flowers and the aureole of spring over the city of Paris. But he was now about to underline his word by means of a prodigy, in order that everyone should be fully convinced of his real and efficacious presence.

She spoke, and in the blink of an eye, the sun was covered, the hall was plunged into darkness, a rumble filled it and lightning sprang forth. At the height of the ceiling a dazzling sword and a crown of light formed momentarily, and then disappeared.

Again light returned, the sky cleared, and calm was reestablished.

A few members of the assembly had dispersed, frightened, while women had screamed. Everyone hastened to assure Marie Fleuriot that they were all convinced, and would dispense henceforth with any prodigy.

Then Marie spoke.

"The Almighty has chosen me as his unworthy messenger, in order that you might hear his will from a human mouth. Any other more immediate manifestation of God would, in fact, be incompatible with the weakness of your bodies. His aspect could not be supported by human eyes. Similarly, it is in order not to alarm you too much, in order not to snatch you violently from your habits, that he allows himself to be called God. He has instructed me to tell you that in reality, he is neither Jehovah, nor Buddha, nor any of the other phantoms that the world worships. As for what he is in verity, it is necessary that we despair of grasping or imagining that, since humans only think and represent things by comparison and analogy. We only advance in knowledge by means of the memory of things already seen and experienced. Nevertheless, although he is not as we imagine him to be, God approves of all idols. The essential thing, he says, is worship; from the moment that the Divine can be represented in reality—since, once again, it is impossible to conceive the inconceivable—it matters little whether he is designated under he named of Brahma or Vishnu, Mohammed or Allah."

Noel Lloyd, who appeared profoundly disconcerted, asked what name He wanted to be given.

MARIE

The Unnamed pleases him well enough. He also admits the Eternal, since that says a great deal to poor human brains.

NOEL LLOYD

And how should he be represented, for preference?

MARIE

As everything that is—that is the most appropriate representation and the only one that is really admissible. Everything that is: a leaf, a tree, a child's smile, a beautiful poem, a sunset, a dolor, a joy. Everything that is, *and something more*.

NOEL LLOYD
What attributes is it necessary to give him?

MARIE
The attributes that you judge the rarest, and which cost you the most to merit them yourselves. Call him Just, Clement. Merciful, Devoid of Passions. All that is agreeable to him, for all that shows that you are granting him what you conceive as the best. Know nevertheless that he is neither particularly inclined to pity not particularly benevolent, given that he created evil and pain, and introduced them as necessary elements to the whole. It is with the aid of pain that he moves the world and makes it progress; and he is himself an ocean of dolor. As for his justice, it is only apparent when one embraces the totality of things. It is a unique justice, composed of a sequence of particular iniquities. It will only burst forth in its perfection at the end of cycles, and escapes, in consequence, the partial sight of humans.

NOEL LLOYD
I don't understand.

MARIE
God accords you the comprehension.

Let us note in passing that, from that moment on, Noel Lloyd began to comprehend everything, and by virtue of that fact, such a change took place within him that those who knew him no longer recognized him.

Then, Marie expressed herself henceforth to anyone and, in enunciating directly the divine word, explained the reasons that had determined the Almighty to manifest himself.

MARIE

The Earth had ended up making too much racket with its prayers and plaints. In order to believe, it experienced the need to see its creator, and, in order to make contact with him, it demanded a miracle. I had, however, from the beginning, formed the worlds in such a way that any ulterior intervention would be unnecessary. It was false to conclude that my impassivity implied my nonexistence. The Earth bears its future within itself, which it develops gradually. In my design, it was the creature itself that ought to modify its destinies, making fructify slowly and patiently the seeds of good will, liberty and amour that I had enclosed within it primitively. For millions of years I have not judged it necessary to interfere with the actions and reactions produced in the bosom of worlds. In the same way that your microbiologists abandon their test tubes to repose in order that the cultures might multiply and prosper, I left spheres and expansions of life to pursue their development.

Nevertheless, I have wanted today to deviate from my habits and fulfill your persistent and pressing prayers. It has pleased me that, for once, the unhoped-for might be realized, the impossible accomplished. And here I am, ready to satisfy your requests. It is the war that was the object of your lamentations. I have made it cease, thus altering the pre-established march and perturbing the sequence of events.

Voices burst forth in the assembly: "Abolish war definitively!"

"Abolish all struggle from our universe!"

"Make human cease killing their fellows!"

MARIE

I descended among you to grant your wishes. I repeat, therefore, that your prayer will be heard, although it would seem to me more worthy if it were the intimate consciousness of your fraternal bonds that softened and extinguished struggles and dissensions rather than an external intervention. But may your wish be realized. You ask that war disappear? You only see the evil that it brings, because that evil is immediate. Your short sight only embraces the present. What I would have liked to be sure of is that you sincerely desire universal peace. For I believe I see that the kings, the financiers and the military men are only formulating that wish reluctantly. Only the mothers and fiancées are speaking without afterthought. Already, the Americans are deploring the end of the struggle, for they are ambitious to dominate. And if the other peoples aspire to peace, it is only temporarily, and because they recognize that they are less prepared.

But imploring voices rose up again: "Let peace descend upon the Earth!"

"Let the olive-branch become the emblem of the nations!"

MARIE

So be it. Your wish will be granted. But it is also necessary that you measure its exact range, as well as the inconveniences of what you are soliciting. Along with war, it will not only be the rivalry between humans that will cease, but he more general struggle between all creatures. Every being will be considered as sacred, all will have the right to exist, and life will become inviolable.

Sir Oliver Test objected then, in the midst of a approving rumor, that it was necessary for God to permit humans to kill the animals indispensable to their nourishment, and also to exterminate harmful insects and uproot evil plants, in order that prosperity might reign on Earth.

The German dictator van Herskin also stood up and asked that colonial warfare be allowed to subsist, by way of an exception.

MARIE
You are demanding too much partiality. In the beginning, all wars had the form of colonial wars. It was a colonial war that Rome waged against nascent Europe.

Monsieur Jules Vibret, who had chemical knowledge, asked that microbes be left in a state of struggle, otherwise, no substance would any longer be subject to transformation, plants would no longer grow, cadavers would cease to dissolve and life on the planet would soon become impossible. It was entirely necessary, he said, also to maintain the struggle against animals in order that they would not pullulate and render the world uninhabitable.

MARIE
You want, then, to live without conflict in a universe at war? That is an unjust sign, a disruption of the eternal plan. However, I grant it to you.

Joyful cries were heard, acclamations and applause. Marie imposed silence, and went on:

MARIE

Henceforth, wars will cease. No one will be able to insult his neighbor nor supplant him, no one will be able to take possession of another's wealth, no one will be aggrandized at the expense of is brethren. That will change you a great deal, but I have descended to earth in order to render you content. That is why, as well as the cessation of war to which I have consented, I am disposed to realize any other wish emitted by the ensemble of humankind. I intend that my exceptional visitation should satisfy you fully. Provided that your wishes are reasonable, or at least appear so to you, and provided above all that they are presented to me unanimously, I will grant them.

And as several people were already agitating, desirous of speaking and formulating requests, Marie went on:

MARIE

There is no need for haste. A month of reflection is given to the earth. Consult one another, weigh your desires, summarize them, in order only to present the essential ones. On the first day of the month of April I shall descend among you again. Above all, let no one attempt to solicit individual miracles. Only questions of a strictly general order should be submitted to me.

Noel Lloyd, who, henceforth radiant with a superabundance of intelligence, did not forget his electors in Yorkshire, enquired as to whether the wishes ought to be decided by universal suffrage.

MARIE

I am neither a socialist nor a democrat. It is injustice that has necessitated such moderating regimes among you. My plan and my creation are founded on the preponderance of the better. Nature proceeds by selection, and whoever says selection and evolution implies choice and differences. Only the individual who is eminent, rising above others, exists in my eyes. The rest is only spoiled matter. It is in that sense that you ought to listen to the small number of the Elect of which a certain gospel speaks. In the vegetable kingdom as well as that of the animals, in all the ranks of those that march and progress, you can grasp my intentions. If I had wanted to create you equal, I would not have established the immense graduated scale that extends from the ameba to the human, the ascendant hierarchy that forms those that aspire to heights. The multitude does not exist in my eyes, any more than the humus that serves to nourish the plant. For me, the shepherd is preferable to the flock.

NOEL LLOYD

But then, what will become henceforth, in the world, of republics, socialism, and our struggles or equality?

MARIE

Socialism, the struggle for equality—all that could provide guarantees against injustice, but all that will become unnecessary since there will no longer be any competition or oppression, no one to surpass and no longer anyone to flatter, no one to dupe. Do you think that in abolishing war between nations, I would conserve civil war?

Noel Lloyd penetrated by melancholy, stammered: "I comprehend, I comprehend."

It was thus, on the divine promise of a new and final session, that the congress came to an end. If the heads of state went out saddened, seeing their careers terminated and already cursing the untimely intervention of the Eternal, the people, who had heard the great promises, rejoiced, and an immense acclamation toward the heavens welcomed the announcement of the favors that the Almighty had already accorded to the Earth, and those that he would grant subsequently.

The members of the Assembly were carried in triumph, and if Marie Fleuriot did not have her part in that apotheosis, it was because she disappeared, transported to her home supernaturally.

The President of the French Republic manifested the intention of signing her nomination for the Grand-Croix de la Légion d'honneur, and the Académie wanted to elect her among its members, but Marie refused.

People had difficulty believing in that refusal. Divine honors being of recent date, society was astonished that anyone could give them preference over the human.

That evening, Paris was illuminated. On the boulevards, where the flow of people surpassed incomparably that of holidays, the newsvendors were selling caricatures representing Presidents Dusol and Noel Lloyd in conference with God, along with humorous couplets:

We shall have / What we want...

And:

The Good God is smiling, / That's promising, promising...

II

Martigny went home radiant through a Paris that was exultant.

"It's a signal glory for us," he said, "to belong to the distinct and miraculous generation that has conversed with the Lord!"

He took pleasure in observing the expansive faces of the worthy people who filled the streets and who, in the license accorded by the government, were drinking singing and dancing.

"I've never encountered as many drunken people as this evening," admitted Léry, who was walking alongside him. "It's remarkable, all the same, that scarcely do human beings feel happy than they start drinking, as if they wanted to forget their happiness."

Astarot, whom the two friends encountered on the Pont des Arts, had the same impression.

"This reminds me of the fourteenth of July," he said. "Anyway, have we not, in a way, taken the Bastille for a second time? And a supernatural Bastille! Now, it remains for us to reflect on what it's appropriate to request. What an embarrassment! As long as the tongue doesn't betray us, as in a fairy tale, at the moment of the supreme wish..."

When he got home, Martigny found his daughter and his son-in-law on the balcony, in the process if savoring the mildness of the evening.

Maurice, who, in the general forgetfulness of evil, had lost the memory of the horrors of the war, was living an endless honeymoon with Antoinette.

"You haven't been out?" Martigny said to them. "Then you don't know anything of what's happened!"

And, wanting to communicate to them his dazzling impression of everything that the future contained, in his opinion, of hope, he told them about the famous session and the perspectives that were offered to humankind.

"Everything will change," he concluded. "Everything will be transformed. A new life is beginning for the world."

But the two lovers listened without joy. They pressed more tightly against one another and looked at Martigny fearfully.

"So, everything's going to change!" exclaimed Antoinette, regretfully.

"Yes," replied the dramatist. "Human beings can ask for anything they desire: new senses, broader horizons, an unexperienced state of the soul, an incorruptible carnal envelope..."

The young woman's eyes widened. "What a misfortune!" she murmured. "What good will it do?"

"You're mad, Antoinette!" exclaimed Martigny. "One would think that this unexpected news, this joyful announcement, has plunged you into despair..."

"We're so happy, you see," she replied. "Our days go by perfectly. Every hour that comes brings us the plenitude of which we dream..."

"You can always wish for more, though," said Martigny, nonplussed.

"We have nothing to desire. We have everything. Our sole desire would be that the present state of affairs remain unchanged."

"Can you be as happy as that?" said Martigny, seized by the expression of bliss on his daughter's face.

"We're so happy," the young woman affirmed, "that I fear that we'll be less so when everything is transformed."

Without adding another word, Martigny withdrew to his study. He was emotional, as if he had penetrated into a sanctuary.

How great the power of amour is! he said to himself. *It renders the divine sensible and present. It subjugates happiness and appears to confound it with ecstasy. If we desire something and address plaints to Heaven, it's because we no longer possess the passion that transfigures and completes life.*

III

The month of May, which was called the month of reflection, passed in a tumult of debate. Soon, great popular meetings at which the orators formulated contradictory projects, the stormy parliamentary sessions of the two worlds, and, above all, the articles in the newspapers, confused and envenomed the questions marvelously.

However, one would not say that the virulence of the arguments surpassed greatly what was habitually seen in Europe at the time of legislative elections. For, despairing of being able to obtain a personal profit from the divine dispositions, condemned only to ask for the general good, politicians and businessmen became disinterested. Obviously, they still contradicted one another in the Chambre and in popular meetings, but it was mostly by acquired force of inveterate habit, and in order to be slightly disagreeable to former adversaries. In the same way, in the newspapers, through the contradictory projects that succeeded one another, professional antipathies and rivalries were easily discernible.

In the first moment of enthusiasm everyone had fallen into accord to ask God for wealth. An outpouring of gold over the Earth had appeared a sensible and immediate good, all the more so because the war had rendered the metal particularly rare and extremely attractive. Some orators, avid for popularity, had insisted on the benefits that universal prosperity would bring.

But it had been quickly understood that gold, abundantly and equally divided between all, would lose its value and be debased. Furthermore, the leveling of wealth was repugnant to people who were rich by heredity, and had a great aversion to it. Since the origins of the world, those who had prescribed equality had nursed the secret hope of applying it to others while maintaining for themselves the supreme mastery over the equal. As God had said to Noel Lloyd, domination was the keyword of nature entire, the original aspiration, the salt of life, the unique motive.

Thus to the extent that everyone desire to receive money in order to have an advantage over everyone else, the idea of the community of wealth offended pride. That is why the popular leaders soon feigned indignation. They proclaimed that it was necessary not to ask for material goods but for moral goods. It was toward amelioration and liberation that it was appropriate to direct efforts.

The paleographer Léry, who, in spite of the worldwide revolutions, never ceased to remain naïve, emitted the opinion that it was necessary to ask God for Truth.

"What could be more advantageous than banishing lies and errors from the world?" he said, triumphantly.

But that entirely abstract proposal, communicated to the newspapers, received a cold welcome from public opinion.

"You've offended your contemporaries and attracted their disapproval, my dear Léry," Martigny said to him. "So you do not know, then, that truth, put in honor by the science if the nineteenth century, is secretly hated and feared nowadays? People mistrust it instinctively, and for intimate reasons. Not wrongly, moreover, for lying acts like a powerful narcotic on human dolors: lying brings repose, aids one to love, even maintains life. Without it, everything would seem sad and depressing. It was during the last war, especially, that the benefits of illusions and the utter uselessness of the truth became apparent in a flagrant manner. It was by believing themselves victorious, on both sides, in spite of all plausibility, and accusing the adversaries with conviction, by declaring in both camps that they were fighting for civilization and not for petroleum, by attributing all heroism and all virtue to themselves, by telling themselves that they alone were privileged by God, that the Slavo-Germans and the Saxo-Latins alike were able, without revolt and without going out of their minds, to support the disasters of the war. Don't wish for humans the deadly gift of the truth. You'd be the first to be desolated by its effects."

"There are in France, however," Léry replied, "idealistic natures that are orientated toward the search for truth and aspire to its advent."

"The proud and presumptuous natures of which you speak are fortunately very rare," replied Martigny, laughing, "and their example will not be followed."

In time, the proposal of President Fichton, who, by dint of magnifying liberty before his America fellow citizens, had ended up by subjugating them and becoming a sort of lay dictator of the New World, contrived to conciliate all the wishes.

President Fichton proposed to claim from God a benefit of the most general order that would combine money—which is to say, prosperity—and truth, or at least the appeasement that it is supposedly able to provide.

"Ask for happiness," said the statesman. "The other goods accompany happiness like a cortege of slaves. Like a bundle, like a crown, happiness includes all satisfactions."

The American's proposition won a unanimous success and attracted all suffrage.

The same fortune was enjoyed by the journalist Flip, who advised eloquently soliciting immortality from God. Although old and wrinkled, she still desired to live.

"As soon as humans are happy and even beforehand, they desire not to die," said Flip. "They want to endure, and that is their primary, their essential will."

In fact, Martigny thought, *to survive while the flowers wither, while the animals disappear, while the seasons succeed one another, to continue to endure while the centuries go by, suns pale and planets grow cold— still to exist when nothing else any longer exists, when origins are forgotten, when everything has changed—to oppose universal death—is certainly an ardent desire that is common to us all. Unsated by life, repelled by old age, humans aspire to drink from the springs of immortality.*

"No longer to die!" Such was the popular echo stimulated by Flip's wish.

From, then on, by means of huge posters, speeches and numerous articles that second universal wish for immortality was imposed on the Assembly.

Only a few Indians in Tibet and a few Japanese and Russians were opposed to it, claiming that death is only change. They made the observation that life resides in its intensity and not in its duration.

"To accomplish one's destiny," they said, "is the unique goal of existence. Once that goal is attained, to die—which is to say, to be reintegrated into the current of universal harmony, seems to be in conformity with the idea of evolutionary progress and eternal renewal."

But these reflections favorable to death and, by that very fact, antinatural, were stifled by a general cry of disapproval. Immortality was definitely inscribed, along-side happiness on the list of human wishes. Compared with those two essential aspirations, any others appeared superfluous. And it was to satisfy the avid insatiable and irreflective tendencies that the word possessed that the members of the Assembly declared themselves disposed to add a third wish, and that they would institute on that subject a kind of competition.

People therefore continued to reflect, and to discuss. In fact, they discussed incessantly; and, in spite of the sacred union that seemed to conciliate the world with a view to universal wellbeing, voices soon became embittered. In addition to formulating a wish, everyone wanted his personal opinion to be heeded and to prevail.

There were old poets who asked for an eternal spring on the Earth; others, still young, who wanted the pleasures of amour to be sharper and more prolonged; and others, finally, who called for the creation of new suns, unknown perfumes and unexpected flowerings.

"Let Beauty reign over the world!" cried the esthetes. "Let there no longer be ugliness, and let genius by the prerogative of all!"

On the part of scientists, the revelation of the ultimate secrets of nature was demanded.

But the multitude remained hostile to all those projects, which would only satisfy certain privileged individuals and which, in consequence, would not affect them. The popular newspapers described those aspirations as the maneuvers of intellectuals and refined desires, and even went so far as to call them sadistic.

Then a new incoherent crop of proposals succeeded one another. Everyone tried to exaggerate the importance of his own métier and wanted the divinity to favor it.

Music lovers wanted the wind to form natural concerts and that all terrestrial sounds should be regular and rhythmic, in accordance with the laws of harmony.

There were morphine addicts and alcoholics who opined that dreaming ought to reign over humans, since a blissful somnolence was the supreme ideal of life.

Finally, after many quarrels and dissents, a new wish was inscribed on the list of demands. That wish solicited integrity of character for men and virtue for women.

The first part of the demand was suggested by the editor of the newspaper *La Famine*, an anarchist député who, compromised three times in sleazy lawsuits, appealed for the integrity of all in order to restore his own.

As for the second, it emanated from the wife of the advocate Clermont Latouille. Virtuous by lack of temperament and by a blemished complexion, Madame Clermont Latouille wanted to spite other women and simultaneously annoy men by making her condition, devoid of grace or pleasure, a general estate. Hence, and as she was also distinguished by her obesity, she was nicknamed Mama Virtue.

Men deprived of avidity and the temptations of lucre, modest women freed from all carnal curiosity—that was what would achieve perfection on the planet.

And as the newspapers prudently advised that the Eternal not be overwhelmed by multiple and disorderly demands, the list was proclaimed closed.

Since the meeting at the Sorbonne, Marie Fleuriot had sensed that God had quit her and that no breath and no emotion revealed the presence of the Divinity within her. But when people were finally in accord as to what they desired, the prophetess sensed that she was visited again by grace and invaded, as it were, by the supernatural.

On the eve of the appointed day when the Eternal was to hear mortal wishes, she entered definitively into a kind of hypnosis.

One final anxiety now possessed the world. Would the Almighty consent to grant such exorbitant pretentions, which would transform the Earth into a privileged planet, into a kind of eternal paradise devoid of evils, death and effort?

What people feared above seeing refused—that for which they dared not hope—was the gift of immortality. Would not God see in that an excessive ambition on the part of humankind, a desire to equal and scale the heights of Heaven? Then again, Eternity on Earth would render Paradise redundant, abolish Hell and set aside the necessity for recompense and punishment. The future would become a prisoner of the Earth; nothing would remain for the Afterlife.

How could God accept such an overturning of his original design, such a perfect negation of all religious conceptions? Admitting that he might accord happiness, he would never consent to grant immortality as well.

"Unlike the rest of you," said Martigny to the journalist from *Le Temps*, who had me to interview him again, "I'm full of hope. Don't have too much fear of a refusal. God will grant everything, since he has promised that. Furthermore, what will it cost him? It's evident that humans persist in having a paltry idea of him, since they imagine bounds and limits to his power or his will."

IV

The decisive day finally dawned, and the wireless telegraph was ready to transmit the response of the Eternal immediately to the remotest parts of the world.

People assembled, as they had the first time, and what occurred in the great amphitheater of the studious Sorbonne was to remain unforgettable.

Sylvestre Dusol, who had been charged with the difficult mission of formulating the desires of humankind, did so in an emotional voice, after a few well-chosen words containing the anticipated thanks. He hoped, he said, that the Eternal would not be irritated by the height of terrestrial ambitions. If, nevertheless, one of the three demands appeared too audacious, or reckless, not to say unrealizable, he begged the Almighty nevertheless to heed the other two.

Everyone agreed that Sylvestre Dusol was, that day, eloquent, honeyed, flattering and, at moments, sublime. As in the finest days of his youth when he had attracted, by means of his siren song, the votes of electors, he wanted to draw and convince God.

Surprise equaled joy when, at Marie Fleuriot's first words, it was evident that the Eternal accepted.

In fact, Marie replied that God already knew human aspirations before they had been thought. Breaking the common laws, or at least perturbing them, he granted them all, for he wanted humans to cease complaining. That was the reason why he had descended to the Earth.

This is the rest, in the inspired one's own words:

MARIE

From sunrise tomorrow, humans will be happy, immortal, integral and virtuous, in conformity with their desires. And furthermore, I shall leave them the memory of their present state. In that way, they will be in a position incessantly to compare the past with the present, and to sense the differences between life such as I originally granted it to them and life as it will henceforth be.

Léry, who could not believe his ears, exclaimed: "Immortality! Can it be true, Lord, that you are granting us immortality? But that must embarrass you…what will become of your Paradise and your Hell? I'm confused by that"

All gazes were directed toward the man who had committed the gaffe, and a murmur of irritation was heard in the hall.

It was thought that, given that God, on an impulse of generosity, had granted everything, it was excessively maladroit to cause him to measure the extent and the consequences of his concessions. An instant of anxiety reigned in the fall, and everyone feared that the Eternal might regret his decision.

But, as Martigny judged immediately, God, like a human being, had doubtless reflected in advance on the consequences of his actions, and there was no chance that anyone could tell him anything new.

MARIE

There is no Paradise and no Hell, and nothing is capable of hindering or shackling destinies. Let the cries cease henceforth! Let Heaven be troubled no longer by prayers and imprecations! Let Nimrod send fewer arrows on high, and Job fewer complaints!

An acclamation of hectic joy welcomed the solemn divine promise, and many people applauded.

In the blink of a eye, the crowd was informed, and electricity began to spread the joyous news via the airways.

Their wishes granted by the Eternal, human beings were fashioning their terrestrial destiny in accordance with their dreams and desires.

The Golden Age, the truly paradisal life, was about to commence...

PART FOUR: PARADISE REFOUND

I

It seems difficult to explain, with order and consequence, the results of the change that had occurred in human destinies.

First of all, it is impossible to evaluate the duration of the era of bliss. The beginning and the end of it can be clearly distinguished, but one cannot attempt to measure the time elapsed between the two events.

The day after the last supernatural intervention, everything occurred in accordance with the divine promises. Humankind, washed clean of dolor, purified of vice, liberated from death, was plunged into an abyss of felicity. That abyss was profound, Finding themselves within it unexpectedly, the living savored at first the same delightful sentiment of repose that slumber gives in succeeding the fatigues of a difficult day.

What voluptuousness there was in setting down that burden of cares, of no longer having to be preoccupied with the future, assured of keeping eternally that which one possesses! No more necessity for vigilance, efforts or precautions. Warnings of danger, the starts of dolor, the wounds of self-esteem, and the bitterness caused by injustice, were abolished.

Léry was amazed, and paraded his amazement everywhere.

"Eternity," he said, raising his arms to the heavens, "is deployed around us like an endless carpet, a route without reefs. And note that it leaves no purchase for bad luck, to tenebrous malevolence, to perverse suggestion. The surface of an unalterable lake—that is what our life will be henceforth."

And Léry was right.

Everything happened as wished.

The sun rose without an escort of clouds, the rains were brief and gentle. The earth produced a great deal, the trees were continually bent under the abundance of fruits. As for the beasts, they served humans of their own free will, without constraint.

In the early days the artisans worked, but not very much and uniquely out of probity and acquired habit. Soon, they gave up; for a perpetual miracle destined to equilibrate happiness was sufficient for everything, anticipating every desire, setting aside all rivalry, all difficulty, realizing and perfecting every enterprise.

Deprived of hatred and interest, the newspapers diminished rapidly in number, having only items of good news to announce; there were no others.

No one was born, no one died. Social distinctions were effaced. No more politicians, no more priests. No difference between governors and governed. The marvelous hierarchy of nature that ordered the city and graduated it, maintaining the same savant and harmonious inequality that characterized the seven reeds of Pan's flute, had disappeared.

Women steeped themselves in the balms of virtue, while men, without the desire to triumph, to rise above their peers, saw their days go by in an imperturbable tranquility.

"Everything is beautiful!"

"Everything is good!"

"It's perfect!"

Those were the words that human beings exchanged by way of greeting when they met one another on the street. They spoke them in an atonal voice, with no vivacity or fire, for there was no longer any fire or bitterness in the words of the living.

To tell the truth, humankind was somnolent.

And as God had allowed to subsist, by exception, the sense of comparison in the minds of individuals, it was somnolent while being conscious of its torpor.

So, after an immeasurable lapse of time, people began to look at one another as if they had something to say but hesitated to express it. At the hour of waking in the morning, families, friends in the street and in gatherings, confronted one another with embarrassment. Nevertheless, gradually, the boldest ended up opening their thoughts to their intimates.

President Fichton, who had become a simple human among humans, but who retained the memory of his past supremacy, murmured one day in the ear of his wife, who was barely wake, on the nineteenth floor of a building in Chicago:

"Something very strange has happened to me, Eveline. I've wanted to talk about it for some time…"

"What's the matter, my friend?"

"Although I'm not absolutely certain, I think..."

"What do you think?"

"That I'm bored."

"It's possible. I too find tedious this interminable succession of similar days."

"We're in accord, then! I knew that fundamentally, we were in accord. But I beg you, not a word to anyone! We were the leaders and, on the other hand, it was me who pressed humankind to ask God for happiness. It's necessary not to set a bad example now. And then, who knows? Perhaps it's only happening to us..."

In fact, it was happening to everyone. In Chicago as in Paris, people were weary of the new state of things, for one wearies rapidly of that which does not change.

And nothing changed. Soon, in fact, humankind had the stupefaction of observing that, since the miraculous day when God had granted the beneficent regime, everything seemed stationary and time no longer flowed.

People lived continually in the aftermath of happiness. That is because, as a great philosopher of the past—Henri Bergson—had pointed out, duration can only be grasped in diversity, and only perceived as a succession of changes. That which does not vary does not flow. For want of mutation and alteration, eternity is not perceptible to the eternal.

In the same way, the hands of a watch appear to be immobile because we cannot perceive their slow and regular displacement, and the moment of awakening is confused with that of going to sleep, even if the slumber has lasted a thousand years.

Thus, no longer having the sentiment of advancing or being modified, humans believed that they had stopped and were immobile. Assured of lasting forever, they lived without consciousness. Human beings traversed a single moment, incessantly the same, and that moment was mortally indifferent to them.

II

One afternoon, in the home of the novelist Leparfait, who had stopped aging and was satisfied by that, but without that satisfaction being mingled with any vivid pleasure, people were discussing the present malaise.

"We're gathering out of habit," Leparfait complained, "and gathering indolently, idly and without desire. Furthermore, once gathered, we remain bleak, blissful and silent. Where are our eloquent and vehement soirées of old? The men crossed words like swords, while expectation, desire and hatred shone in their faces. The women were the object of covetousness, so the hours passed vertiginously, delightfully. The amour of the flesh and the amour of money incessantly sharpened minds, enabling this salon, in the same way as every other salon, to become similar to a forest on a summer's day, when the birds and insects sing and agitate, competing as to which will obtain the female, the fodder and the nest."

"But what do you expect, my dear friend?" replied Martigny. "It's necessary to resign oneself to it. One can only engage in repartee, shine and surpass one another when moved by desire, pushed by ambition. To be witty is an effort, and every effort presumes a goal."

"You don't mean, I hope, that by virtue of an excess of happiness we've become idiots?" Léry objected, who still had a vague liking for contradiction, but who now contradicted without emphasis or bitterness.

"No, Léry, we haven't become idiots—and I deplore that. Have you not noticed, then, that there are no more idiots any more than there are men of intelligence? Henceforth, there are only satisfied individuals. Happiness has effaced oppositions and contrasts, the beautiful contest of light and darkness. It has leveled everything, sentiments as well as things. It's frightful. My daughter Antoinette told me yesterday that her amour has deflated, devoid of tension. She is not unhappy beside the lover that her husband is, but she no longer experiences either hopes or anxieties, and in consequence, no longer has the sensation of loving and being loved."

"We're too privileged," sighed Leparfait. "God has given us too much."

"I reproach him for it," said Martigny. "Because the advent of permanent happiness and perfect virtue, as well as certain deliverance from death, have taken all the spurs away from life, not only emptying it of all poison but of all effervescence. The absence of danger has annihilated the attractions of risk. Deprived of anxiety, existence becomes, by virtue of that very fact, deprived of hope. Finally, effort, in disappearing, has taken with it illusion, in the same way that pain has taken pleasure with it, and fear tranquility."

That's true," replied Leparfait. "Before, the rare recompense of life resided in the partial realization of our hopes. Unfortunate, storm-tossed, humans experienced the supreme joy of sometimes obtaining whatever they were pursuing. Now that all goals are attained in advance, they necessarily become undesirable. Have you noticed, above all—and it's a frightful thing—that happiness no longer provokes any surprise?"

"The salt of life," Martigny retorted, "the leavens that inflated and expanded existence—glory, amour and lust—have fled the Earth. When do you expect? It was inevitable. In order to aspire to glory, it's necessary that individuals are rivals and in conflict, in the same way that in order to stir passion, it's necessary that they know doubt and anguish. In sum, it's the dolor of not being loved, the panic of seeing a rival preferred to oneself, the effort to vanquish where others have failed—in brief, all those states that are enemies of happiness—which, through an ocean of long vicissitudes and sufferings, prepare the bitter and fugitive happiness of an instant."

"What I regret most of all," confessed Léry, "is the diversity of the passing hours and the unexpected pleasure provided by the sentiment of the route traveled. Alas henceforth, we will no longer see children growing older. What joys and what emotions one felt once in following the blossoming of little blond heads, of seeing beauty come to visit the imprecise features of young women, melancholy maturity conferring a final and mortal attraction to those who, still beautiful, are already in the process of growing old. The days no longer cause my joy, since they're all uniformly perfect. The splendor of sunsets no longer provokes sublime melancholy in my soul, since they can no longer provoke the idea of death. How, henceforth, can we rediscover that supreme acuity of sensation that we experienced before the rare perfect moments of life, telling ourselves that they might perhaps be the last?"

"Let's admit that vice, and also perversion, seem to have taken away, in quitting us, something impalpable and shiny, something comparable to the iridescent powder of a butterfly's wing," said the shrill vice of Baronne Lehmann. "Woman, who was once, like the flower, queen of the terrestrial garden, has lost her seductions, since she no longer thinks of heightening them either by make-up or coquetry. The impossibility of sin, and the definitive installation of virtue, have broken the feminine springs. A man is no longer for us a possible prey, and the idea of dominating him, like that of triumphing over our rivals, has been lost. By virtue of that very fact, we have forgotten all the cunning, all the artifice of beauty. All the fashion magazines have closed down, hairdressers have disappeared and perfumes are neglected. And with them, we have also forgotten the furtive glances, the promising smiles, the gestures that evoke pleasure, the quivering of the nostrils that summons the couch and the embrace—all the innate art of pleasing that, since Eve and the Sirens, drew men into a road of tortures and delights."

"What's prodigious," observed Astarot, "is that husbands, henceforth convinced of the fidelity of their wives, have become indifferent. Sure of not losing them, they scarcely care about them anymore. On the other hand, the young, free vicious women whose presence exalted virtue and rendered it precious and appreciable, no longer generate talk. From the social point of view, nothing appears to me to be more regrettable. Properly speaking, virtue no longer exists. For, in the end, we only take account of the existence of something by virtue of the coexistence of its opposite. Without vice, there's no virtue, in the same way that without pain, there's no pleasure, and without the fear of death, no pleasure in living."

"Where are we going? Where are we going?" exclaimed Leparfait, raising his arms to the heavens in a sign of protest and perplexity.

"We aren't going anywhere, and that's what's despairing," Martigny replied, tranquilly, as he picked up his hat. "To go implies an intention to arrive, and arrival signifies an end. Now, we're immortal. We have no end or goal. Durable, we're immobile. But at least, for today, we can go to bed!"

III

Humankind soon arrived at losing the estimation of everything.

What had been remarked in the home of the novelist Leparfait became universally graspable. In the same way that a mortal idleness had succeeded the futility of all effort, and the absence of danger had taken away the sense of courage and heroism, the certainty of being able to obtain what one wished had abolished the charm and surprise of realizations and destroyed illusion.

Humans perceived that they no longer loved, that they no longer desired. Young, they felt in their hearts the chill of old age. They had lost curiosity—the supreme stimulant of life—as well as the appetite for knowledge. For we only learned with a view to improving ourselves, of getting ahead of others, of attaining the object of our ambition.

"Do you know, my friend, that I now go along the street without anyone looking at me or any man following me" lamented Madame de Fleurus, stopping Astarot in front of the Louvre museum, which no one visited any longer.

"Don't complain, Madame," the astronomer replied. "Far graver things are happening nowadays. You say that no one any longer notices you in the street, and already that's bad. But have you not observed that the stars revolve in the heavens without anyone studying them, that flowers bloom in the fields without anyone picking them, that the days go by without exciting any regret and the seasons succeed one another without provoking pleasure? Henceforth, humans no longer experience either dread or amazement. By virtue of that fact, one might say that they do not see, nor feel, not hear."

Progressively, the memory of the past that God had left them caused humans to conceive immense regrets.

"Where are our amours and our delicious emotions? How can we rediscover our troubles and our anguish, as well as struggling against forbidden desires and temptations?"

Suddenly, a cry went up:

"What's the point of living?"

And shortly thereafter, the cry was completed:

"What's the point of living, since we can't die?"

"Well, they're right! Martigny said to himself, amused. "And yet I never perceived it. In fact, its death that gives life its price. Death alone accords its proper value to each instant. It invites us to hasten to enjoy, and to exhaust, the present moment and hope and fear for the future by turns."

What people regretted the most, after amour, was the delight of the old days—the lost sentiments of repose, awakening and convalescence that followed fatigue, dolor and mourning, and provide I know not what illusion of rebirth.

The Princesse de Clairval, the poet, wrote a lyrical piece on the subject of Dolor, certain fragments of which were soon on everyone's lips:

"O Dolor," she sang, "divine Dolor, who marked our efforts and appeared to measure our forward march, who created great things and ennobled us, enriched us and refined us! Dolor, instrument of all progress, of all ascension, come back! Retrace your steps swiftly and bring with you the brief moments of respite, the repose that we called joy, all our vanished treasures!"

It was as if humans were disinherited, wandering idly, since no one struggled and no one had any desire to surpass others or to surpass themselves.

"If we added up our accounts," said Leparfait, "We'd discover that we've lost everything. Where are our difficulties, our uncertainties, and also our hopes that were born of our doubts? Where is the sublime spur that incited us to work in order to leave something behind us and thus escape forgetfulness and also death—the death that confers on all things their price and their value, by virtue of the very horror and dread that it inspires?"

IV

One day, Astarot came running, in panic, to Martigny's house.

In his haste he had forgotten to put on a waistcoat and had stuffed on his head a straw hat that gave his attire a strange aspect in the middle of winter.

"I'm scared," he said, letting himself fall into an armchair, "I don't know if you're in the same state, but for myself, I can't doubt it: my senses are weakening. Yes, Martigny, my faculties are getting feebler from day to day. The clarity of my vision, the acuity of my hearing, my delicacy of taste and touch, all those proven and vigilant companions that aided me to enter into contact with nature, to monitor it, to avoid its ambushes, to preserve myself against its ruses, are diminishing and seem to be going away!"

"Naturally," Martigny replied. "You've taken a long time to perceive it, my dear Astarot, "which proves, not meaning to displease you, that your perceptions have never been very vivid. It shouldn't surprise you, in any case. Isn't it explicable that our senses are etiolating in inaction? We no longer look, we no longer listen, why should we give ourselves the trouble, since the roads are safe, the animals tamed, since it's unnecessary to avoid what one does not fear or to attempt to perceive that for which one no longer hopes?"

At that moment Antoinette came into her father's study.

"Have you read Marie Fleuriot's article?" she asked. And, on his negative response: "I've brought it for you. More clear-sighted and more spontaneous than any of us, Marie is uttering the first cry of protest."

She unfolded a very small printed sheet.

"I didn't know that the newspapers still persisted in appearing," said Astarot.

"Only *Le Temps* still has the courage," Martigny replied. "A shrunken *Temps*, no longer measuring more than twenty centimeters, whose title no longer expresses any meaning."

"Read us Marie Fleuriot's article, then," Asked the astronomer. "I'm curious to see whether she's in accord with our thoughts and sentiments."

Antoinette read:

"What use is it to us to be immortal if we are dying incessantly, if our life is nothing but an endless old age, a perpetual lethargy, a motionless death? Who would not give up their immortality for a single minute of old, one of those minutes filled with terror and expectation, of patience and pain, in which, supporting the present, we calculated and lived in anticipation of the future? It is lost, the holy and beautiful fatigue of the laborer returning from the fields and heading toward the desired repose. Lost also are the sublime resurrections when, once malady and death had been averted, we enjoyed with delight all the spectacles and all the sensations that lived within us. What has become of the injustice that rendered justice sacred, the human failings and human sins delectable to commit and so voluptuously bitter afterwards by virtue of the remorse they bring?

"Everything is accessible to us now, everything succeeds in our hands, everything completes us. And yet, our condition is more lamentable than that of beggars and starvelings. No shelter henceforth for an illusion, no motive for hope. There is no sacrifice any long-

218

er, since no one suffers. Every impulse is broken and, an aggravating and supreme symptom, prayer has been extinguished on our lips. What is the point of praying, since we no longer expect anything? Nobility itself has disappeared from the earth, for where could a foundation be found for it, when there is no more suffering or abnegation?"

"The article is excellent," opined Astarot. "It measures well the gulf into which we have fallen voluntarily. But if Marie Fleuriot says clearly where we are, she doesn't say how we can get out of it—that, however, is the capital point."

V

Protestations and regrets similar to those expressed by Marie began to be heard everywhere. They translated the universal sentiment.

Someone referred to the life of old as *The Lost Paradise*, and now that expression flourished on all lips. *The Lost Paradise!* Thus was crystallized, in memory, the old world of dolor and ordeals—the world of evil and of death, of vice and of perversity, the world in which people struggled, hated one another, suffered injustice, endure privation, succumbed to disease, were crippled by injury—the world of cries, plaints and lamentations, the world of revolt and inequality.

The Lost Paradise!

People aspired to it again without daring to hope, having regret for everything that had been, including the unhappiness that, increasingly, was surrounded by an indescribable aureole.

Fortunate Death…holy Dolor…sweet Vice: such were the names that were given to the scourges of old. People had finally understood that evil is only abhorred and detested while it is in the presence of good, and that happiness and immortality lose all value by virtue of their isolation, which prevents their comparison with unhappiness and death, and by that very fact, their esteem.

"Fortunate are those who have died, since they have existed!" cried human beings now. "Fortunate are those who suffered, since they subsequently had the notion and consciousness of their brief joys, while we persist, unconsciously, in the monotony of our immortality."

Hesitant and timid at first, and then more tenacious, these plaints rose up toward Heaven...

The world appealed for its deliverance; humankind wanted to be relieved of the nightmare of happiness.

When people wanted to formulate the aspirations, wishes and desires of all, they had recourse to Martigny.

"We want," the latter specified, "quite simply, to go back, to reintegrate with the past, to feel once again the asperities of life, to wound ourselves on its thorns, to experience once again the tortures of fear, to rediscover that which was redoubtable in the beauty of women and the joys of drunkenness. And above all, we want to be ignorant of the future and to be able to challenge it."

On the advice of Marie Fleuriot, unanimous prayers were addressed to Heaven from all lands, vehement prayers, participating in complaint and revolt.

"God, give us Death, take away perpetual Happiness, anoint us with the holy oils of Dolor, enable all of us no longer to be equal in order that we might strive, that we might act; awaken us immediately to hope and illusion! Let our breasts swell with anxiety and the gentle dew of tears spring from our renewed eyes! *Render us the divine faculty of measuring time.* And in order that we find it brief and fugitive, have us visited by its sister Destruction! Let the sublime décor of risks, contrasts and changes return to envelop the Earth, enfevering the perspectives of the world! To be born amid dolor, to taste an infinity of pains and a few moments of delightful joy, to have incessantly the terrifying consciousness of the passing of the hours...*to die! to die!*"

Such were the prayers frenetically ejaculated in churches, in books, and in newspapers.

Those prayers contained the dream of the Earth. Poets composed "Odes to Death" and demanded the rejuvenation that war provokes, while novels inspired nothing but the evocation of the evils of yore, past anguishes and vanished torments...

"In sum, Papa, if we're still living, it's only by means of memory," Antoinette said to Martigny. "The shadow of our former adventures, the reflection of our precarious days of old—that's what God permitted us to conserve, and they are our sole delights. Without that, our burial would be absolute."

"Let's hope, my child," replied Martigny. If God has left us the memory, it's doubtless because he has no intention of abandoning us."

In fact, when the prayers were unanimous and regret had united all hearts, the Eternal became manifest.

A violent storm was unleashed in the skies of Europe, which had remained equally serene for a long time.

Then hearts palpitated with joy, and an immense hope was born in human beings.

The following day, Marie Fleuriot confirmed the expectations:

"God," she said, "consents to lend his audience once again to the prayers of the Earth. For the last time, he will descend among us."

And the messenger felt herself traversed once again by the divine will and Word.

VI

This time, the supernatural session took place austerely, without excitement and without tumult. People were ashamed and perturbed. They recognized that they were at fault. They had ended up being conscious of having committed a kind of indiscretion, no longer personal or social but cosmic, transcendental and celestial.

There was little preliminary discourse, immediately ceding the floor to Marie. Sylvestre Dusol, and then Noel Lloyd with his white beard, his absent forehead and horizontal face, remained as representatives of the old world, alongside the former President of the United States, whose shiny clean-shaven face was reminiscent of a parchment devoid of letters and meaning. And the three augurs looked at one another, silently and atonally. Noel Lloyd was even more somber than the others for, by virtue of the divine intervention, he had begun to understand and had become discreet. Having lost his loquacity, he was manifestly awkward in his movements.

The Eternal declared that he would lend a favorable ear for the third time to the confused and changing aspirations of his creatures. He consented that humankind would be replaced in the former beaten track and that its original destinies would resume their course and their efficacy.

Life would flow as before, the miracle would be effaced and nothing—not even the memory—would subsist of the ephemeral era of Happiness and Immortality.

The Assembly then wanted to pour out actions of grace and celebrate the return of the eternal ordeals with the same ardor with which they had celebrated their disappearance. But God repressed those whims severely.

MARIE

There is no need to thank me. Furthermore, your gratitude will not last long. Soon, you will start to complain again and resume solicitation. For the need for the new, the desire for what one does not have—ferments that I placed in your hearts in order that you would be incessantly incited to progress—inevitably become sources of a perpetual discontentment. In truth, it is a lesson that I have given you in granting you what you demanded, in order to demonstrate to you, that the only true help for you is within yourselves. You wishes have been granted, the miracle has served you as a slave. Nevertheless, my benefits, which surpassed the most ancient and most audacious of your hopes, have quickly become a cause of ennui and sterility for you. It is necessary that you resign yourselves to comprehending that only the slow transformation of the human heart can serve humankind. It is there also that you must seek the cessation of war. Unfortunately, your short lives poison you with perpetual desires and generous aspirations that do not last.

In those recent times you hated suffering and sought the despicable mediocrity of equal happiness. That which is rare, and which is only precious because of its rarity, you wanted to be abundant, without reflecting that once it has become abundant, it ceases to be appreciated. In that, felicity is comparable to gold. Scattered and precarious, difficult to attain, it is enviable. Abundant, stable and without the possibility of its disappearance, it is contemptible. In the same way, you wanted immortality, as if the delicious taste of days that flee the thirst to prolong them, the bitter sensation of living and enjoying life did not obtain their aliment from the omnipresence of Death.

"How, above all, were you able to believe that any perturbation in the general design could be fortunate? You misunderstood the essential notion, and even seemed to be unaware that humankind is only one infimal voice in the universal plurimondial concert, and the earth a tiny candle in the vast stellar glare. It is in that respect that the prayer, the wish, everything that humankind formulates, in daring blindly to desire anything other than what happens, is the most puerile and the most lamentable of absurdities of your petty universe.

Thus spoke the Eternal. And he spoke for a long time, developing the cosmic harmonies and showing that everything only exists by contrast and only lives by opposition, that the evils and difficulties of which humankind would be delivered would simultaneously deprive them of the corresponding goods. Even that which is called life, he said, is in reality only a unilateral aspect of a phenomenon. "Like the light and dark that, by their opposition and their alliance compose all terrestrial images and figures, so Evil and Good, Life and Death, Love and Hate, form the varied and marvelous fabric of things down here. There is no landscape without shadows, since it is the shadows that render visible and appreciable the luminous accidents. And there is no existence without tears, which form the relief and trace the bounds of joy."

The Eternal would have continued to speak in that way, but he doubtless perceived that people were only paying attention to him out of deference and were understanding him poorly. The members of the Assembly were incessantly caressing the hope of soon being reintegrated in the joyous diversity of old. And in thinking about that, they became incapable of thinking about anything else

It also happened that, Time having instantaneously resumed its empire, one of the members of the said Assembly—the microbiologist Arnicroff, who had wished more ardently than all the others for the advent of Happiness and then the return of Dolor—had a heart attack while the Eternal was speaking.

No one thought of bringing him help, but everyone took at it as the proof and the seal of the divine promise. Arnicroff, who was old, thus passed imperceptibly from life to death.

That visitation of Death, for which humankind had ceased to hope a long time ago, was celebrated as a happy event. Cries of triumph rose up on all sides. People gathered hastily around the cadaver in order to make sure that the return of the great renovator was real. The entire assembly was jubilant. Humans could die, then henceforth! It was not an illusion; true life was recommencing.

When the emotion had calmed down, the Eternal terminated his discourse by warning the representatives of humankind that it was his last appearance.

For millions of centuries the Earth would roll though celestial space without any further manifestation of a particular will.

MARIE

Nevertheless, in order to leave you a pledge of my intervention, a tangible and incontestable souvenir of my descent among you, I will not attenuate Dolor or retard

Death—which would be deceptive benefits—but I will revive the freshness of your sensations, communicate a new vigor to your emotions before dawns and sunsets, the immensity of the sea, before amour and youth, before flowers and spring. By slowing the march of science and civilization, I will bring you a little closer to Nature, I shall efface the kind of senility that knowledge and experience bring. The down of puberty, the mantle of innocence of which you have deprived yourself and which you discarded some time ago: that is what I shall reestablish.

On the other hand, I will attenuate the corrosive doubt, the poison of uncertainty that paralyzes your will and renders you decrepit. And furthermore, I will abolish in you the knowledge of recent destructive inventions. You shall no longer fly, the equal of the birds, since you have only profited from wings to sow death from a greater height and more rapidly over your peers. You shall no longer kill except with the aid of the honest dagger, and henceforth you shall present your breast to the enemy when you declare war, in order that you can see in advance the face of the man you are murdering. You will be deprived of the insidious compositions of unstable elements that have permitted you to produce immense deflagrations and plagiarize celestial lightning.

In brief, I will render you a little youth and I will take away, efface from your hearts, the wrinkles and make-up of decadence. Strive, above all, to gaze at the Universe not in order to profit from it but in order to reintegrate with it as your natural bosom. Remember that every dagger plunges into flesh that might be fraternal and that every cry of pain that you provoke corrupts and destroys something in your own soul. Finally, in order to be immortal in the sole fashion that is accessible to human beings, try to live on after death in future memories by means of a trace of good. As a final grace, I am doubling the seed of bounty that I put into your essence originally. Try to make it sufficient.

Such was the supreme vestige of the message of the Eternal among mortals.

Life resumed joyfully. But that joy, although durable, did not last indefinitely.

At first humans lived submissively, meekly welcoming the little joy and the infinity of pain that life brought. They shivered at the sight of beautiful spectacles and cared little about death, instinctively lingering on savoring the present moment. Their relative ignorance and the spontaneity of their sensations, the virginity of the heart that the Eternal had rendered them, caused existence to unfurl like a beautiful dream. In sum, evil was tolerated, injustice passed almost unperceived.

Nevertheless, gradually, by virtue of the patience and ineluctable force of progress, thought returned to produce its ravages. Humans began to reflect again, and in reflecting, recognized their misfortune. Becoming conscious of their dolors, they wanted to number them, complained of them, and launched arrows toward the Eternal. Philosophers came to doubt his existence, and certain new exegetes of religious history claimed that, in reality, the world have been visited not by God but Satan, and that it was really a supreme temptation that humankind had traversed.

In moaning and thinking, humans acted. The further they advanced along the road of speculation and knowledge, the more amour lost its attraction.

Natural marvels struck their senses less and only struck melancholy chords. Regretting dying, human beings declared strife barbaric and death inhuman.

And the peoples began making war on one another again. They made war in the ancient manner, face to face, iron in hand. Victory was proportionate to the strength of their muscles. No sacrifice and no satanic intervention appeared as yet to favor one of the adversaries.

But soon, as ideas continued to progress incessantly, after poetry and philosophy, science made its reappearance.

A monk who was fond of chemistry, prayed little and devoted his time to bizarre experiments, succeeded in producing a black paste composed of sulfur, saltpeter and carbon, which detonated curiously when one set fire to it. The said monk filled a metallic tube with it, which, with the aid of a burning wick, exploded destructively.

The king of the land had the impious solitary blown up on a barrel of his diabolical powder, but the discovery continued to be exploited nonetheless, and shortly afterwards, cannons were manufactured. Subsequently, other inventors succeeded in multiplying the force of the new powder tenfold.

And the nations that, for a long time already, had resumed moaning against war, recommenced practicing it *en masse*, furiously and conscientiously.

SF & FANTASY

Adolphe Alhaiza. *Cybele*

Alphonse Allais. *The Adventures of Captain Cap*

Henri Allorge. *The Great Cataclysm*

Guy d'Armen. *Doc Ardan: The City of Gold and Lepers; The Trog-lodytes of Mount Everest/The Giants of Black Lake; The Abominable Snowman*

G.-J. Arnaud. *The Ice Company*

André Arnyvelde. *The Ark; The Mutilated Bacchus*

Charles Asselineau. *The Double Life*

Henri Austruy. *The Eupantophone; The Olotelepan; The Petitpaon Era*

Barillet-Lagargousse. *The Final War*

Cyprien Bérard. *The Vampire Lord Ruthwen*

S. Henry Berthoud. *Martyrs of Science; The Angel Asrael*

Aloysius Bertrand. *Gaspard de la Nuit*

Richard Bessière. *The Gardens of the Apocalypse; The Masters of Silence*

Chevalier de Béthune. *The World of Mercury*

Albert Bleunard. *Ever Smaller*

Félix Bodin. *The Novel of the Future*

Pierre Boitard. *Journey to the Sun*

Louis Boussenard. *Monsieur Synthesis*

Alphonse Brown. *City of Glass; The Conquest of the Air*

Émile Calvet. *In a Thousand Years*

André Caroff. *The Terror of Madame Atomos; Miss Atomos; The Return of Madame Atomos; The Mistake of Madame Atomos; The Monsters of Madame Atomos; The Revenge of Madame Atomos; The Resurrection of Madame Atomos; The Mark of Madame Atomos; The Spheres of Madame Atomos; The Wrath of Madame Atomos* (w/M. & Sylvie Stéphan)

Félicien Champsaur. *Homo-Deus; The Human Arrow; Nora, The Ape-Woman; Ouha, King of the Apes; Pharaoh's Wife*

Didier de Chousy. *Ignis*

Jules Clarétie. *Obsession*

Jacques Collin de Plancy. *Voyage to the Center of the Earth*

Michel Corday. *The Eternal Flame; The Lynx* (w/André Couvreur)

André Couvreur. *Caresco, Superman; The Exploits of Professor Tornada* (3 vols.); *The Necessary Evil*

Gaston Danville. *The Perfume of Lust*
Camille Debans. *The Misfortunes of John Bull*
Captain Danrit. *Undersea Odyssey*
C. I. Defontenay. *Star (Psi Cassiopeia)*
Charles Derennes. *The People of the Pole*
Georges Dodds (anthologist). *The Missing Link*
Charles Dodeman. *The Silent Bomb*
Harry Dickson. *The Heir of Dracula; Harry Dickson vs. The Spider*
Jules Dornay. *Lord Ruthven Begins*
Alfred Driou. *The Adventures of a Parisian Aeronaut*
Odette Dulac. *The War of the Sexes*
Alexandre Dumas. *The Return of Lord Ruthven; The Man who Married a Mermaid* (w/P. Lacroix)
Renée Dunan. *Baal; The Ultimate Pleasure*
J.-C. Dunyach. *The Night Orchid; The Thieves of Silence*
Henri Duvernois. *The Man Who Found Himself*
Achille Eyraud. *Voyage to Venus*
Henri Falk. *The Age of Lead*
Paul Féval. *Anne of the Isles; Knightshade; Revenants; Vampire City; The Vampire Countess; The Wandering Jew's Daughter*
Paul Féval, *fils. Felifax, the Tiger-Man*
Charles de Fieux. *Lamékis*
Fernand Fleuret. *Jim Click*
Charles-Marie Flor O'Squarr. *Phantoms*
Louis Forest. *Someone is Stealing Children in Paris*
Arnould Galopin. *Doctor Omega; Doctor Omega and the Shadowmen* (anthology)
Judith Gautier. *Isoline and the Serpent-Flower*
H. Gayar. *The Marvelous Adventures of Serge Myrandhal on Mars*
Louis Geoffroy. *The Apocryphal Napoleon*
G.L. Gick. *Harry Dickson and the Werewolf of Rutherford Grange*
Raoul Gineste. *The Second Life of Doctor Albin*
Delphine de Girardin. *Balzac's Cane*
Léon Gozlan. *The Vampire of the Val-de-Grâce*
Jules Gros. *The Fossil Man*
Jimmy Guieu. *The Polarian-Denebian War* (2 vols.)
Edmond Haraucourt. *Daah, the First Human; Illusions of Immortality*
Nathalie Henneberg. *The Green Gods*
Eugène Hennebert. *The Enchanted City*
Jules Hoche. *The Maker of Men and His Formula*
V. Hugo, P. Foucher & P. Meurice. *The Hunchback of Notre-Dame*

Romain d'Huissier. *Hexagon: Dark Matter*
Jules Janin. *The Magnetized Corpse*
Gustave Kahn. *The Tale of Gold and Silence*
Gérard Klein. *The Mote in Time's Eye*
Fernand Kolney. *Love in 5000 Years*
Paul Lacroix. *Danse Macabre; The Man who Married a Mermaid* (w/Alexandre Dumas)
Louis-Guillaume de La Follie. *The Unpretentious Philosopher*
Jean de La Hire. *The Fiery Wheel; Enter the Nyctalope; The Nyctalope on Mars; The Nyctalope vs. Lucifer; The Nyctalope Steps In; Night of the Nyctalope; Return of the Nyctalope*
Etienne-Léon de Lamothe-Langon. *The Virgin Vampire*
André Laurie. *Spiridon*
Gabriel de Lautrec. *The Vengeance of the Oval Portrait*
Alain le Drimeur. *The Future City*
Georges Le Faure & Henri de Graffigny. *The Extraordinary Adventures of a Russian Scientist Across the Solar System* (2 vols.)
Gustave Le Rouge. *The Dominion of the World* (w/Gustave Guitton) (4 vols.); *The Mysterious Doctor Cornelius* (3 vols.); *The Vampires of Mars*
Jules Lermina. *The Battle of Strasbourg; Mysteryville; Panic in Paris; The Secret of Zippelius; To-Ho and the Gold Destroyers*
Maurice Level. *The Gates of Hell*
André Lichtenberger. *The Centaurs; The Children of the Crab*
Maurice Limat. *Mephista*
Listonai. *The Philosophical Voyager*
Jean-Marc & Randy Lofficier. *Edgar Allan Poe on Mars; The Katrina Protocol; Pacifica 1, 2; Robonocchio; Return of the Nyctalope;* (anthologists) *Tales of the Shadowmen 1-13; The Vampire Almanac* (2 vols.)
Ch. Lomon & P.-B. Gheuzi. *The Last Days of Atlantis*
Camille Mauclair. *The Virgin Orient*
Xavier Mauméjean. *The League of Heroes*
Joseph Méry. *The Tower of Destiny*
Hippolyte Mettais. *Paris Before the Deluge; The Year 5865*
Louise Michel. *The Human Microbes; The New World*
Tony Moilin. *Paris in the Year 2000*
Michael Moorcock's *Legends of the Multiverse*
José Moselli. *Illa's End*
John-Antoine Nau. *Enemy Force*
Marie Nizet. *Captain Vampire*

Charles Nodier. *Trilby and The Crumb Fairy*

C. Nodier, A. Beraud & Toussaint-Merle. *Frankenstein*

Henri de Parville. *An Inhabitant of the Planet Mars*

Gaston de Pawlowski. *Journey to the Land of the 4th Dimension*

Georges Pellerin. *The World in 2000 Years*

Ernest Pérochon. *The Frenetic People*

Pierre Pelot. *The Child Who Walked on the Sky*

Jean Petithuguenin. *An International Mission to the Moon*

J. Polidori, C. Nodier, E. Scribe. *Lord Ruthven the Vampire*

P.-A. Ponson du Terrail. *The Immortal Woman; The Vampire and the Devil's Son; The Police Agent*

Georges Price. *The Missing Men of the* Sirius

René Pujol. *The Chimerical Quest*

Edgar Quinet. *Ahasuerus; The Enchanter Merlin*

Henri de Régnier. *A Surfeit of Mirrors*

Maurice Renard. *The Blue Peril; Doctor Lerne; The Doctored Man; A Man Among the Microbes; The Master of Light*

Restif de la Bretonne. *The Discovery of the Austral Continent by a Flying Man; Posthumous Correspondence* (3 vols.); *The Fay Ouroucoucou* (2 vols.)

Jean Richepin. *The Crazy Corner; The Wing*

Albert Robida. *The Adventures of Saturnin Farandoul; Chalet in the Sky; The Clock of the Centuries; The Electric Life; The Engineer Von Satanas*

J.-H. Rosny Aîné. *Helgvor of the Blue River; The Givreuse Enigma; The Mysterious Force; The Navigators of Space; Vamireh; The World of the Variants; The Young Vampire*

Marcel Rouff. *Journey to the Inverted World*

Marie-Anne de Roumier-Robert. *The Voyage of Lord Seaton to the Seven Planets*

Léonie Rouzade. *The World Turned Upside Down*

Han Ryner. *The Human Ant; The Superhumans*

Louis-Claude de Saint-Martin. *The Crocodile*

Frank Schildiner. *The Quest of Frankenstein; The Triumph of Frankenstein*

Pierre de Selenes: *An Unknown World*

Norbert Sevestre. *Sâr Dubnotal: Vs. Jack the Ripper; The Astral Trail*

Angelo de Sorr. *The Vampires of London*

Brian Stableford. *The Empire of the Necromancers (1. The Shadow of Frankenstein; 2. Frankenstein and the Vampire Countess; 3. Frank-*

enstein in London); The Wayward Muse; Eurydice's Lament; The Mirror of Dionysius; The New Faust at the Tragicomique; Sherlock Holmes and The Vampires of Eternity; The Stones of Camelot (anthologist) *News from the Moon; The Germans on Venus; The Supreme Progress; The World Above the World; Nemoville; Investigations of the Future; The Conqueror of Death; The Revolt of the Machines; The Man With the Blue Face; The Aerial Valley; The New Moon; The Nickel Man; On the Brink of the World's End; The Mirror of Present Events; The Humanisphere*

Jacques Spitz. *The Eye of Purgatory*

Kurt Steiner. *Ortog*

Eugène Thébault. *Radio-Terror*

C.-F. Tiphaigne de La Roche. *Amilec*

Simon Tyssot de Patot. *The Strange Voyages of Jacques Massé and Pierre de Mésange*

Louis Ulbach. *Prince Bonifacio*

Théo Varlet. *The Castaways of Eros; The Golden Rock.; The Martian Epic* (w/Octave Joncquel); *Timeslip Troopers* (w/André Blandin); *The Xenobiotic Invasion*

Pierre Véron. *The Merchants of Health*

Paul Vibert. *The Mysterious Fluid*

Villiers de l'Isle-Adam. *The Scaffold; The Vampire Soul*

Gaston de Wailly. *The Murderer of the World*

Philippe Ward. *Artahe; Manhattan Ghost* (w/Mickael Laguerre); *The Song of Montségur* (w/Sylvie Miller)

Victor Margueritte. *The Bacheloress; The Companion; The Couple*

MYSTERIES & THRILLERS

M. Allain & P. Souvestre. *The Daughter of Fantômas*

A. Anicet-Bourgeois & Lucien Dabril. *Rocambole* (stage plays)

Guy d'Armen. *Doc Ardan: The City of Gold and Lepers; The Troglodytes of Mount Everest/The Giants of Black Lake; Doc Ardan: The Abominable Snowman*

Cyprien Bérard. *The Vampire Lord Ruthwen*

A. Bernède. *Belphegor; Judex* (w/Louis Feuillade); *The Return of Judex* (w/Louis Feuillade); *The Shadow of Judex* (anthology)

A. Bisson & G. Livet. *Nick Carter vs. Fantômas* (stage play)

André Caroff. *The Terror of Madame Atomos; Miss Atomos; The Return of Madame Atomos; The Mistake of Madame Atomos; The*

Monsters of Madame Atomos; The Revenge of Madame Atomos; The Resurrection of Madame Atomos; The Mark of Madame Atomos; The Spheres of Madame Atomos; The Wrath of Madame Atomos (w/M. & Sylvie Stéphan)

Félicien Champsaur. *Homo-Deus; Nora, The Ape-Woman; Ouha, King of the Apes*

Jules Clarétie. *Obsession*

V. Darlay & H. de Gorsse. *Arsène Lupin vs. Sherlock Holmes: The Stage Play* (stage play)

Harry Dickson. *Harry Dickson vs. The Heir of Dracula; Harry Dickson vs. The Spider*

Séamas Duffy. *Sherlock Holmes in Paris*

Alexandre Dumas. *The Return of Lord Ruthven* (stage play)

Paul Féval. *The Black Coats (The Parisian Jungle; Heart of Steel; The Sword-Swallower; 'Salem Street; The Invisible Weapon; The Companions of the Treasure; The Cadet Gang); Gentlemen of the Night; John Devil*

Paul Féval, *fils. Felifax, the Tiger-Man*

Louis Forest. *Someone is Stealing Children in Paris*

Émile Gaboriau. *Monsieur Lecoq; The Casebook of Monsieur Lecoq*

Arnould Galopin: *Harry Dickson: The Man in Grey; Harry Dickson: Tenebras*

Goron & Émile Gautier. *Spawn of the Penitentiary*

G.L. Gick. *Harry Dickson and The Werewolf of Rutherford Grange*

Léon Gozlan. *The Vampire of the Val-de-Grâce*

Georges Grison. *The Heads that fell in Paris*

Paul d'Ivoi. *Around the World on Five Sous* (w/Henri Chabrillat)

Paul Lacroix. *Danse Macabre*

Jean de La Hire. *Enter the Nyctalope; The Nyctalope on Mars; The Nyctalope vs. Lucifer; The Nyctalope Steps In; Night of the Nyctalope; Return of the Nyctalope*

Rick Lai. *Shadows of the Opera: Retribution in Blood; Sisters of the Shadows: The Curse of Cagliostro*

Etienne-Léon de Lamothe-Langon. *The Virgin Vampire*

Steve Leadley. *Sherlock Holmes and The Circle of Blood*

Maurice Leblanc. *Arsène Lupin vs. Countess Cagliostro; Arsène Lupin vs. Sherlock Holmes (1. The Blonde Phantom; 2. The Hollow Needle); The Island of the Thirty Coffin; 813; The Many Faces of Arsène Lupin* (anthology)

Gustave Lerouge: *The Mysterious Doctor Cornelius* (3 vols.)

Gaston Leroux. *Chéri-Bibi* (stage play); *The Phantom of the Opera; Rouletabille & the Mystery of the Yellow Room; Rouletabille at Krupp's*

Maurice Limat. *Mephista*

Jean-Marc & Randy Lofficier. *The Katrina Protocol;* (anthologists) *Tales of the Shadowmen 1-13; The Vampire Almanac* (2 vols.)

Richard Marsh. *The Complete Adventures of Judith Lee*

William Patrick Maynard. *The Terror of Fu Manchu; The Destiny of Fu Manchu*

Frank J. Morlok. *Sherlock Holmes: The Grand Horizontals* (stage play); *Sherlock Holmes vs Jack the Ripper* (stage play); *Sherlock Holmes, Fantômas, Lupin, Raffles and More: The Spanish Plays* (stage plays)

Jean Petithuguenin. *The Adventures of Ethel King, The Female Nick Carter*

P.-A. Ponson du Terrail. *The Immortal Woman; The Vampire and the Devil's Son; The Police Agent*

Georges Price. *The Missing Men of the* Sirius

Charles Rabou: *The Secret Bureau: 1. The Secret Bureau; 2: The Brothers of Death*

Antonin Reschal. *The Adventures of Miss Boston, The First Female Detective*

Norbert Sevestre. *Sâr Dubnotal vs. Jack the Ripper; The Astral Trail*

Eugène Thébault. *Radio-Terror*

P. de Wattyne & Y. Walter. *Sherlock Holmes vs. Fantômas* (stage play)

David White. *Fantômas in America*

Pierre Yrondy. *The Adventures of Thérèse Arnaud of the French Secret Service*

NON-FICTION

Stephen R. Bissette. *Blur 1-5. Green Mountain Cinema 1; Teen Angels*

Win Scott Eckert. *Crossovers* (2 vols.)

Georges Grison. *The Heads that Fell in Paris*

Jean-Marc & Randy Lofficier. *Shadowmen* (2 vols.)

Randy Lofficier. *Over Here*

Brian Stableford. *The Plurality of Imaginary Worlds*